ALSO BY RICHARD PAUL EVANS

The Christmas Box
Timepiece

✳ RICHARD PAUL EVANS ✳

THE Letter

SIMON & SCHUSTER

This Large Print Book carries the
Seal of Approval of N.A.V.H.

SIMON & SCHUSTER
Rockefeller Center
1230 Avenue of the Americas
New York, NY 10020

SIMON & SCHUSTER and colophon are
registered trademarks
of Simon & Schuster Inc.

Manufactured in the United States of America

1 3 5 7 9 10 8 6 4 2

Library of Congress Cataloging-in-Publication Data

Evans, Richard Paul.
The letter / Richard Paul Evans.
p.   cm.
I. Title.
PS3555.V259L48   1997
813'.54—dc21   97-34444
                                                             CIP

ISBN 0-684-84283-1

✦ A C K N O W L E D G M E N T S ✦

t has been said that an author's mind is like a magician's hat—you cannot take out what was not first put in. With such consideration I acknowledge my debt to the following: C. S. Lewis, Dr. Viktor E. Frankl, Dr. M. Scott Peck, and Neal A. Maxwell. May their words continue to light our tenebrous paths and lighten our journeys.

I again thank my Lauries: my editor, Laurie Chittenden, for her insight and quiet heart, and my wunderkind agent, Laurie Liss, for everything; Brandi Anderson for her research assistance, and JoAnn Bongiorno of Chicago's Drake Hotel for her hospitality and research assistance. With great sadness I bid a fond farewell to my dear friend and personal assistant, Celeste Edmunds—one of the original Christmas Box dreamers and bracelet wearers. Thank you for your years of love and service, Cel. Godspeed.

And, always, my sweetheart, Keri, for her grace and dignity. And the three little girls who make my world turn.

SHARE: Pregnancy and Infant Loss Support, Inc., offers support to parents who have lost a baby through miscarriage, stillbirth, or early infant death. For more information please call: 1-800-821-6819.

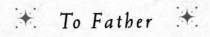 *To Father*

✦ CONTENTS ✦

Contents

. . . these dark days will be worth
all they cost us if they teach us that our true
destiny is not to be ministered unto but to
minister to ourselves and our
fellow men.

✦

—FRANKLIN DELANO
ROOSEVELT
First Inaugural Address, March 4, 1933

✦ PROLOGUE ✦

It was with ardent horror that primitive man first witnessed a solar eclipse—the sun devoured by the predator moon until its light ceased and darkness fell upon the face of the land. The aborigine, too, fell upon the land, crying for the loss of heaven's fire and fear of everlasting night.

We, their more enlightened posterity, have also suffered eclipses. Some, as those in the Dark Ages, endure for centuries, while others pass in blessed brevity. I am not certain if it is the crisis or the uncertainty of its duration that causes the human spirit its greatest anguish, stirring men to cry out to the faceless heavens, "How long, Lord? How long?"

One such eclipse was the darkness that befell the world that black October of 1929 christened in the annals of history as the Great Depression. Commencing with the stock exchange's collapse in New York City, there was scarcely a corner of the globe that did not feel the tremor of that institution's great fall or the bleak chill of its darkness.

The bitterness of the era may only be fully known by those who felt its desperation as banks foreclosed, then folded themselves, leaving millions unemployed, homeless, and hopeless.

But among the tales of despair are also stories of quiet heroics; corner grocers extending credit they know will never be repaid, and landlords overlooking rent until finding themselves faced with destitution. It is often during the worst of times that we see the best of humanity—awakening within the most ordinary of us that which is most sublime.

I do not believe that it is circumstance that produces such greatness any more than it is the canvas that makes the artist. Adversity merely presents the surface on which we render our souls' most exacting likeness. It is in the darkest skies that stars are best seen.

During these days of darkness, in one small corner of the earth—a cemetery in the Salt Lake Valley—a letter was found at the snowy base of an angel monument that marked the grave of a little girl.

I discovered the letter in the winter of 1949 pressed between the pages of a diary that belonged to the child's father, and, at first glance, I regarded it of little consequence. It was only after I had read the diary that I learned of the letter's great significance and the events it set in motion.

The diary—the last volume of a series of leather-bound books which documented the lives of David and MaryAnne Parkin—came into my possession shortly after the death of MaryAnne. Her husband, David, had died fourteen years previous.

MaryAnne Chandler Parkin was a beautiful Englishwoman with the sad, clear eyes of one who has touched the flame of life and learned from its heat. Even in her autumn years she remained beautiful, though, in retrospect, I am not sure if her beauty was entirely physical or induced of the dignity and grace that permeated her being. Whatever the truth, MaryAnne personified compassion—and love makes all comely.

My wife, Keri, and I had, for a season, shared the mansion with the kindly widow up until her passing on the eve of Christmas of 1948. Those were winter days not to be forgotten.

From the soliloquies of David Parkin's diary, I learned a great truth about life—and all relationships—that even the greatest of loves may shudder beneath the shadow of eclipse. I believe that the story of David and MaryAnne is, simply, a love story, though not in the fanciful romanticism of poets and pulp novelists. I am not a believer in love at first sight. For love, in its truest form, is not the thing of starry-eyed or star-crossed lovers, it is far more organic, requiring nurturing and time to fully bloom, and, as such, seen best not in its callow youth but in its wrinkled maturity.

Like all living things, love, too, struggles against hardship, and in the process sheds its fatuous skin to expose one composed of more than just a storm of emotion—one of loyalty and divine friendship. Agape. And though it may be temporarily blinded by adversity, it never gives in or up, holding tight to lofty ideals that transcend this earth and time— while its counterfeit simply concludes it was mistaken and quickly runs off to find the next real thing.

✦

This is the story of David and MaryAnne Parkin's love.

CHAPTER 1

The
Graveyard
Encounter

"The sexton is a peculiar man, enslaved by the dominion of ritual and constancy. His vocation is well chosen as nothing is so reliable as death."

DAVID PARKIN'S DIARY.
JANUARY 29, 1934

SALT LAKE CITY CEMETERY, 1933

As the graveyard fell dark into the shiver of the canyon's breath, the sexton, with the arduous motion of arthritic hands, donned his coat, hat, and scarf, lit the wick of a candle-lantern, then emerged from his cottage into the snow-draped graveyard to chain the cemetery's gates against the threat of grave robbers. Only once, at the outset of his forty-seven-year tenure, had a grave in the cemetery been plundered, but he had decided then that his grounds were in peril and the sexton was a creature of habit in thought as well as observance.

The old man started northwards, up the snow-banked street, until, atop a moonlit knoll, the silhouette of an angel statue came into view against the velvet backdrop of night. The statue had been erected over the grave of a three-year-old girl, the only child of a wealthy Salt Lake City couple, David and MaryAnne Parkin. It had become a landmark in the cemetery and a signpost of the sexton's routine, who, two decades earlier, had changed his daily ritual in this one regard—to commence his morning tour of the grounds from east to west to avoid the child's mother weeping at the foot of the monument.

To his astonishment, as he mounted the knoll, he discovered the woman crouched at the base of the statue. He thought the scene peculiar, for as long as the site had graced his cemetery, the child's beautiful mother had never visited her grave past dusk.

He advanced more slowly, hoping his lantern's dim light or his crunching footfalls would divulge his presence without startling the woman, who, immersed in her grief, was ignorant of both. He stopped, five yards removed, as the snow fell silently around and between them. He impatiently lifted his pocket watch by its fob, dangling it within the light of the flickering lantern, replaced it, then, his routine threatened, loudly cleared his throat— his breath clouding before him in a fog.

The bowed head rose.

"Mrs. Parkin, I must be closin' the yard."

The form moved stiffly, struggling to her feet. To the sexton's surprise it was not the graceful, slender form of the child's mother, but instead the withered and heavyset personage of a woman, older than himself. Her steel-hue hair, framed by a vermilion kerchief, was matted against her forehead, and the lantern's light reflected off the residue of tears which streaked her cheeks. Bewildered, she turned to look at him.

"Excuse me, ma'am. I thought you some other body . . ."

Her grey eyes widened.

". . . 'tis after dusk, I must be closin' up the grounds."

The woman nodded slowly, then wiped her cheeks with an open palm. "I'll go now," she said in a voice as haggard as her appearance. She turned again to the angel, and her hunched shoulders rose and fell with a deep sigh.

The sexton looked down at the monument's granite pedestal at the woman's offering: a single crimson rose atop an envelope.

"Will the trolley board again tonight?"

"Last run to the end of the line at nine forty-five." He glanced again to his pocket watch. "You've twenty minutes, yet."

"Thank you," she muttered, as she dropped her head and started off, shuffling through shin-deep snow, leaving a wide trail between the stone and wood grave markers, until she disappeared into the deeper shadows of a grove of mourning willows.

Without further consideration, the sexton continued his routine, reaching the north gates six minutes and thirteen seconds past his usual schedule.

✦

"Unlike myself, MaryAnne frequently visits our daughter's grave—oftentimes with weekly regularity.

I do not know what she finds in the ritual, nor the particulars of its observance, but at her return her eyes are swollen and her voice spent. It is a reminder of the grief I have unearthed in her life and so deeply buried in mine. I would say that each day the expanse between our hearts widens, except that I cannot be certain.

At such great distance it is difficult to perceive the increase of a few extra yards."

DAVID PARKIN'S DIARY. OCTOBER 11, 1933

❖

MaryAnne Parkin stood before the marble angel nearly as still as the statue itself. Her laced, leather boots were buried past her ankles in a crystalline blanket of crusted snow as a light fall continued to descend. The dawning sun lit the statue in a burgeoning crescent, illuminating half its face and robe—leaving the sculpture divided as a waning moon. A cascade of foot marks, preserved from previous visits, flowed and ebbed from the statue, gathered at its base in a single depression. MaryAnne was aware that not all of the prints were hers, for as she entered the cemetery she had encountered the sexton who had told her of the elderly woman he had, two evenings prior, found kneeling at the angel and mistaken for her. She had not given the sexton's account much consideration, as her mind was filled with thoughts of greater consequence.

She felt as if her heart would break.

"Good-bye, sweet Andrea," she whispered. "I do not know if I shall ever return."

She shuddered at the finality of her words, then lifted a gloved hand to brush back a fresh onset of tears. "I have prayed and prayed for answers. I don't know why God is so silent. I am sorry if I have failed you, but the silence from the two I love most I cannot bear. I know of no other way."

She lowered her head and sobbed until her body shook.

MaryAnne could not recall when she had first considered leaving her home. The notion had, perhaps, attended her daughter's funeral, waiting patiently among the congregation of mourners. But it was not until she had fully felt the estrangement of the man she loved that the notion became real.

The sexes do not deal with tragedy in like manner, and while woman and man may differ in response on many of life's weightier issues, the disparity is far less forgiving in this unhappy realm. Where MaryAnne had outwardly worn her grief as she did its raiment—the veils and cloaks of death's rituals—David had buried his, secreted it away in dark recesses behind stoic walls that widened daily. But walls, emotional or otherwise, are not particular and hold out more than just what they are erected for. In the construction of his walls, David had sequestered more than his pain, but also his love, MaryAnne.

MaryAnne had told no one of her planned escape, as she had continually procrastinated the painful confession for an opportune moment. As the years had relinquished to hours, she realized that there was no opportune moment to share such tidings and now reconsidered telling her husband, as he was certain to entreat her to stay—a request she did not know if she could deny. For the last three years, MaryAnne had viewed herself as one helplessly stranded on the edge of a towering precipice delaying the inevitable leap until the wait had become more painful than the fall she avoided. The event of her brother's wedding in England had provided the ideal opportunity for her departure. It was time to jump.

It was moments later, as she raised her eyes, that she first noticed, on the snow-blanketed shelf of the monument's pedestal, a wilted green stem protruding from the snow. She slowly crouched forward, her petite, gloved hand grasped the flower, raising it to her nose—it was a rose, its bud closed tightly and encrusted in the frost that both killed and preserved. Looking down, she noticed that the flower was not the only occupant of the shelf. Something lay beneath it. She brushed back the snow, uncovering an envelope. The envelope's seal was pressed in burgundy wax, the embossed image of a rosebud, its thorny stem and leaves swirled about the icon in an elaborate flourish. Lifting it from the base, she slid back its flap, extracted its contents, and unfolded parchment as fragile snowflakes lit on the paper, melted, and joined the ink in constitution.

MaryAnne gasped.

Pressing the note to her breast, she glanced

furtively around the silent yard, though it was evident that the letter had endured the freezing night and snowfall. The yard was, as it was always at dawn, vacant of all but its usual breathless inhabitants. She pulled her scarf tighter around her neck and chin, lay the rose at the angel's feet, then stowed the letter in the besom pocket of her fur-lined jacket.

She glanced one last time into the angel's face, then retraced her steps down the knoll and through the west bend of the cemetery where a small wooden gate, fastened between stone supports of weathered brick and mortar, opened to the road which ran in front of the home she prepared to flee.

CHAPTER 2

Lawrence

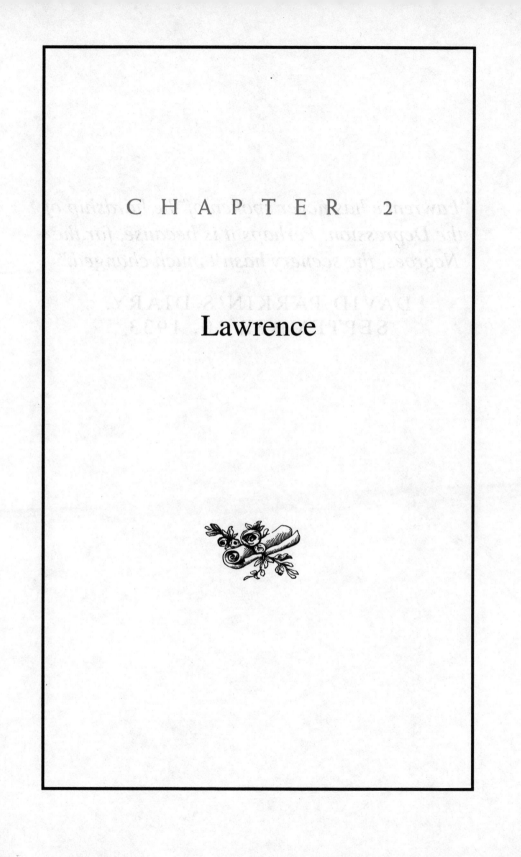

"Lawrence has never spoken of the hardship of the Depression. Perhaps it is because, for the Negroes, the scenery hasn't much changed."

DAVID PARKIN'S DIARY.
SEPTEMBER 10, 1933

As MaryAnne returned from the cemetery, in another part of town, the Parkins' housemaid, Catherine, called on the home of a friend of the Parkin family—an elderly black man named Lawrence Flake.

At the gentle rap, Lawrence turned towards the door though he was unable to see it. Lawrence was blind, his eyes fogged over, in part from age, but chiefly from a cruel December night, twenty years previous, when four men, wild with vengeance and alcohol, had entered the black man's shack and savagely beat him, leaving him for dead. Not an hour later, the same men, led by a brutish miner named Cal Barker, had set fire to the Parkin Mansion, resulting in the death of their three-year-old daughter Andrea. Lawrence had long outlived that tragic night, and two years earlier passed the milestone age of eighty. Had it been within his power, he would gladly have given his years to the little girl.

At the turn of the century, Lawrence Flake was a buffalo soldier serving with the twenty-fourth regiment of the Negro U.S. Cavalry; a commission he held until, at the age of fifty, he retired from the military and settled where it had left him, in the inclement bowl of the Salt Lake Valley.

Most of his years in the military had been spent as troop supply and requisitions clerk, a duty he acquired after demonstrating unusual proficiency in the repair of wagons and rifles. It was here where he had mastered the art of clock repair—the vocation he continued after his discharge. Although he could no longer repair or build clocks, his home was still full of them: some collected with great deliberation, while others he adopted after their owners, most of whom had died years earlier, had abandoned them.

In daily ritual, Lawrence wound the chime clocks, for if he could not see their faces he could still hear their voices, though the custom was practiced for habit, not necessity. At his age and station, he was emancipated of the clocks' tyranny—ate when he was hungry and slept when he was tired. The one exception to his hourless routine was the morning call of Catherine. She came to Lawrence's shack with such constancy that one could set a clock by her visit.

"Come in, darlin' girl," Lawrence shouted. "The ancient, ol' man is waitin' for you."

Catherine pushed open the warped door and entered, preceded by a rush of winter air. The chill braced the small shack, repelled only by the hissing fire in the cast iron belly of the Franklin stove. Her cheeks were rosy from the drive and from the crook of her arm hung a straw basket. She did not remove her coat.

"Good morning, old man. I have brought apple dumplings and ash-pone."

Lawrence sniffed the air, then expelled a loud sigh of pleasure. "Still hot from the oven. Got no reason to envy royalty, Miss Catherine. You take such fine care of me."

His benefactress smiled as she lay the basket on the table. She never doubted her service was appreciated.

"If you would stay at the house I could take better care of you."

"Like I always say, Miss Catherine, Parkins don't need an old, blind Negro sittin' around their place like some piece of broken furniture."

"You are the most stubborn man," Catherine replied, as she set about her morning routine. She extracted a wide-mouthed jar of buttermilk and a bottle of absinthe from her basket and set them both on the table. She unscrewed the cap from the bottle of green liqueur, then twisted the lid off the milk. "Here's your milk."

"That ain't from no bovine."

Catherine smiled. "Mr. Parkin thought you might need a little something."

"David's a right generous soul. You know President Roosevelt done a smart thing in re-peelin' Prohibition, just wish he'd done it 'fore the revenuers got to my stash. Had a whole crate saved for my weddin' or my funeral. Never intended to wet the ground with it."

Catherine emptied the rest of her basket then sat down across from Lawrence as he slowly felt around the table, familiarizing himself with the articles set before him.

"Both Mr. and Mrs. Parkin have said how nice it would be to have you stay at the house. I wish you would consider their invitation. There is plenty of room."

Lawrence's expression grew somber. "It's a hard thing, miss. No doubt David and MaryAnne be sincere in their askin'. No matter where I'm livin' they be takin' care of me. Sometimes I think it might be nice, too, 'specially the way I put you out comin' all the way to my house each day. Feel truly sorrowful 'bout that."

"It is no trouble, Lawrence."

"Just somethin' 'bout a man's castle. No matter how humble that castle be."

He reached for the bottle of absinthe, and Catherine pushed it within his grasp. He ran his fingers up the bottle's neck, then, discovering its cap absent, raised the bottle to his lips, swallowed, then wiped his mouth with his sleeve. "Truth is, won't be much longer when no one need fret over me."

"Don't talk that way."

"Didn't mean no offense by it. Just, man knows when his time's a comin'. Somethin' inside like a clock windin' down."

"I am not one to frequent cemeteries," Catherine rejoined. "In my mind or otherwise. Just foolishness, talking about death."

"I ain't got no problem with dyin', Miss Catherine, it's one of life's simpler things. Like nightfall, it don't require no decision." He paused for Catherine's reprimand, but she said nothing. "Just as well. What use's a horologist that can't see? Been my philosophy that if life ain't useful it ain't nothing. I met people still breathin' that been dead going on twenty years or more. Only difference between them and the stone-cold is a headstone and six feet of dirt." Lawrence paused again, sensing his benefactress's unusual quietness. "You all right this morning, Miss Catherine?"

"I am just a little sad. MaryAnne is leaving tomorrow for England and will be gone until Christmas. It's the first time she's been away so long."

"What's MaryAnne doing in England?"

"Her brother Ethan is getting married."

"Lord and butter. Ain't he a bit old to be settlin' down?"

"We're almost the same age. You'll make me feel like a spinster talking like that," Catherine mused.

Lawrence grimaced, embarrassed by the faux pas. "Sorry, Miss Catherine, didn't mean nothin' by it. Just makin' talk."

A clock chimed the quarter hour, reminding Catherine of the day's obligations. She stood, pushing her chair back by her motion. "I best get back to the house. I have much to do to prepare for MaryAnne's journey."

She gathered the containers back into her basket. "Is there anything else you need?"

Lawrence's voice lowered. "No thank you," he said. "Now don't you go worryin', I won't go talkin' 'bout death like that no more. Least not when you're 'round. Didn't mean to get you upset."

"It's all right, Lawrence." She stopped at the door. "I wrapped the ash-pone for your supper. I will see you tomorrow."

"Tomorrow," he echoed. "My thanks."

He waited for the door to shut before he cussed himself out for offending his day's only visitor.

❋

Through stained and embossed windows, the sweet light of the winter morning lit the mansion's capacious foyer, finding MaryAnne sitting on the second step of the curved stairway. In one hand she held the letter she had just discovered at the angel, her forehead in the other, deliberating the dilemma the letter presented. Catherine's return through the front entry momentarily startled her from her thoughts.

"Good morning, Mary."

"Good morning, Catherine."

Catherine set her basket on the marble floor and, after brushing the snow from her shoulders, commenced to unbutton the vestment. "I have brought out your cases. I left them in the hallway outside the boudoir. I thought I would consult you before I began your packing."

"Thank you, dear."

"What time does your train depart?"

"Tomorrow, before noon. I must be to the station by ten." She rose, concealing the letter at her side. "Were you home when David left?"

"I saw him off a few moments after you went out."

MaryAnne took Catherine's hand and led her to the adjacent drawing room where both women sat on the same velvet love seat, their knees touching. MaryAnne brushed back a threatening tear, removed the letter from its envelope, and handed it to Catherine.

"This morning I found this letter at Andrea's angel."

Catherine unfolded the letter and read it. A perplexed expression blanketed her face. "Is it from Cal Barker?"

MaryAnne hesitated. "I don't think so. It was left with a rose. I believe it is from David's mother."

Catherine gasped. What little she knew of David's mother was unpleasant. David's mother, Rosalyn King, had been a music hall singer when she met Jesse Parkin, a prospector in Grass Valley, California. When David was only six years of age, Rosalyn, having grown weary of the hard life, followed the sirens of celebrity and abandoned her small family to return East to pursue her career on the stage. Thirteen years after her departure, Jesse's dig, the Eureka mine, surrendered one of the richest veins in California history. Jesse Parkin died just two years after the find, leaving twenty-one-year-old David the sole heir of the fortune.

When Rosalyn learned of her former husband's death, she returned to David's life, urging him to send money and come to her in Salt Lake City. Alone, and covetous of family, David immediately forgave his mother, purchased, unseen, the Salt Lake City mansion for the two of them, and impetuously sent ahead twenty-five thousand dollars for the home's furnishings, which Rosalyn immediately absconded with, leaving only a note of her intention to return to Chicago to resurrect her career. She had not been heard from since.

Catherine was only seventeen when she had first met David. She had been left at the mansion by her former employer to watch over the house until its purchaser's arrival. She had nonchalantly delivered the message of Rose's departure, unaware of the pain her news would invoke. Even then, though just newly acquainted with the young David, she could not help but feel empathy for his pain and enmity towards his cruel mother. This morning's reference to the woman sounded peculiar, like a character from a history textbook.

"David's mother?" Catherine repeated. "She is still alive?"

"It is possible." MaryAnne took up the letter and slid it back into the envelope. "I do not want David to see this. I cannot bear that she hurt him again."

"She is an awful woman. It is incomprehensible that she would abandon him."

The words were not intended for MaryAnne, but pierced just as deeply.

"Its arrival at this time is so peculiar," MaryAnne said.

Catherine received her words unable to comprehend their full meaning. "Perhaps you should wait until your return to show him."

The suggestion evoked pain, and MaryAnne's gaze dropped back to the letter. "That is what I'll do." Her words hung in silence as she opened the drawer of a cherry-wood lamp table to hide the letter inside.

"Are you all right, MaryAnne?"

MaryAnne forced a smile. "Anxious for my journey I suppose."

Catherine leaned into her friend's shoulder. "I feel the same. I do not think we have been apart for more than a few days since you and David wed." She sat back. "I am being silly. It is only eight weeks. You will be home before Christmas." She looked into MaryAnne's face. ". . . it is just that you are my best friend."

MaryAnne pulled Catherine closer until her chin rested on the crown of her head, and gently stroked back her hair. "I am weary of good-byes" was all she said. MaryAnne could not believe that a heart that had been through as much as hers could still hurt so.

MaryAnne's
Departure

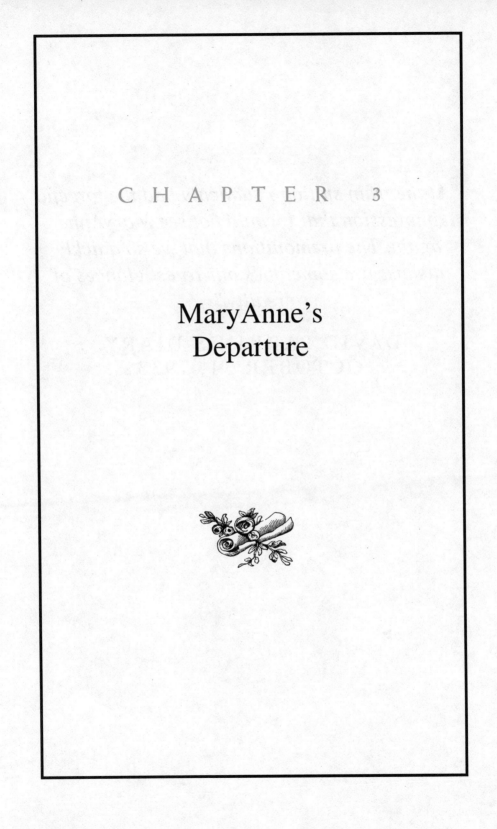

"At the train station I suddenly had the forceful impression that I would not see MaryAnne again. The premonitions that we so quickly dismiss are sometimes our truest glances of reality."

DAVID PARKIN'S DIARY.
OCTOBER 31, 1933

MaryAnne lay awake beneath the bed's comforter when David entered the darkened bedroom at a quarter hour past midnight. She was well aware of the time, as the dozen strikes of the mantelpiece clock had only served to heighten her anxiety of his return. For the past several hours she had awaited the moment in growing trepidation—rehearsed her announcement, anticipated his response, then rehearsed again.

He undressed in the darkness.

"David . . ."

MaryAnne's gentle voice drew his eyes to the bed as he searched for her silhouette.

"I am glad that you are still awake."

He lay his clothes across the back of a nearby chair, then sat on the edge of their bed. "I have been thinking all day about your leaving. I wish you were not traveling alone . . ."

"I will be all right."

"I noticed something peculiar about your tickets. The steamliner was only fifty-three dollars. A round-trip should be twice that. Are you certain your passage is booked correctly?"

"I thought I would not reserve the return trip until I was in England and certain of how long I need stay . . ."

He was appeased by the explanation, which further saddened her. There was a time when he would not have let her travel so far alone. David lay back next to her, pulling the sheets up to his chest.

"David . . . I . . ." Her voice, as her courage, faltered. David rolled over towards her.

"What is it, Mary?"

There was so much to say and nothing she could. She leaned her head into his chest. "Could you just hold me tonight?"

✦

MaryAnne woke a full hour before the dawn. The room's drapes had not been drawn, and the moonfall's luminance cast the room in indigo hues, projecting shadows of the bedposts' spires against the opposite wall. She lay especially still, looking at her sleeping husband, and wondered at how extraordinary the ordinary is rendered when in its final expression. She lay close to him, feeling the warmth of his body and the soothing rise and fall of his chest. There were mornings when he left early for work that she would roll to his side of the bed to feel his lingering warmth pressed against her chest and face. She would never again wake to this man or share his bed. When she could bear the thought no longer she climbed from their berth, slipped off her nightgown, and drew a bath.

She bathed long, powdered and dressed slowly in an effort to fill each moment as full as she could to choke out the pain of the pending day. Not until she heard Catherine's movement downstairs did she descend.

In a daily ritual of more than twenty years, she was drawn to the den and her Bible. The room's fire blazed. It was Catherine's first obligation of the day, a self-appointed task, to start the fire for MaryAnne. MaryAnne took her Bible down from the cherry-wood bookshelf—an aged, Gothic book with an intricately embossed leather cover and gold-edged pages—the most beautiful of the rare Bibles that David had collected in the last several years. She carried the book to her chair, opened to the ribbon marker, then read and wept and read again. Forty minutes later she carried the book out to the kitchen where Catherine was chopping walnuts with a butcher's blade, rolling the wide steel blade in easy motion against a marble breadboard. At MaryAnne's entrance, she turned to pull the drape against the glare of the morning sun.

"Good morning, Catherine. It smells wonderful."

"I am making sweet bread for your journey."

MaryAnne touched her arm. "You are always so thoughtful."

Catherine sprinkled the nuts over the bread, then placed the pan in the oven while MaryAnne lay the Bible on the counter, poured herself a cup of peppermint tea, and carried it to the table.

"I hope you have good weather for your journey. Especially for the ocean liner."

"Especially the ocean liner," MaryAnne repeated. "I get queasy on the rowboats at Liberty Park."

"There is nothing worse."

David entered the kitchen soon after, barefooted and wearing a flannel robe. He was unshaven and his hair was tousled.

"You woke early," he said to MaryAnne.

"It must be the travel jitters."

"Then they are contagious. I tossed and turned all night." He glanced at the Bible, then over to Catherine. "What confection are you about, Catherine?"

"Sweet bread for MaryAnne's journey."

She brought his coffee over to the table. He lifted the cup and looked to MaryAnne.

"Are you all packed?"

MaryAnne answered softly. "I think I have everything."

"You didn't leave your Christmas list."

"It's only October."

He winked. ". . . I need time for these things."

"I will think about it on the train."

He took an envelope from his robe's pocket and set it on the table in front of her. "I think you should carry more money. Just in case."

"I have ample."

". . . Just in case."

She acquiesced, leaving the envelope where it lay.

"How long has it been since you've seen Ethan? It has been nearly twenty years hasn't it?"

"Nearly twenty . . . since Andrea."

"He'll be an old man," David mused. He thoughtfully sipped at his coffee. "Did you recall what you wanted to tell me last night?"

"Last night?"

"You started to tell me something."

She gazed at him for a moment, then took a sip of her tea. "No."

Catherine spread a knife of apple butter across a slice of the hot bread, then brought it over to the table.

MaryAnne suddenly stood. "I had better check my trunks once more."

"Would you like some help?" Catherine offered.

"I am just looking them over." She took the envelope from the table, then slid it between the pages of the Bible and carried both out of the room.

"What time does Mary's train board?" David asked.

"Ten-ten."

David glanced at his watch, then quickly downed his coffee and rose. "I'd better dress."

✦

As the dawn sun stretched above the crest of the Wasatch range, David carried two leather cases from the foyer, followed out by MaryAnne, who paused to take a long look at the house, then silently walked out to the car. She was dressed in heavy winter clothing, a knit, gray wool dress beneath a sable coat that fell to her ankles. A wide-rimmed, felt hat covered the paisley kerchief that concealed her ears and tied beneath her chin. The strap of a leather bag draped across her shoulder.

Catherine emerged a moment later carrying a woven basket filled with sweet bread, sandwiches, and fruit, all bundled within a red, checkered cloth. They stood together a few feet from the automobile while David finished placing the trunks in the back. Catherine handed her the basket.

"I made you some snacks for the train. Walnut sandwiches and ladyfingers. And the sweet bread. I don't suppose the food will be like home."

"I don't suppose it could be."

"Would you like me to see you off at the station?"

MaryAnne shook her head. "Good-bye here is good. I would like to spend some moments alone with David."

Catherine nodded with understanding. Mary-Anne set the basket on the ground and lifted from her handbag an ivory, linen envelope sealed with a gold wax imprint. Across its face was scrawled in her own hand, *My heart.*

"Will you place this in the drawing room next to David's armchair?"

Catherine thought it curious that MaryAnne did not just deliver the letter to David herself, but took the envelope. "I'll deliver it as soon as you are off." She added, "You know, David will miss you dearly."

She smiled sadly. "I know he will."

"Will you write upon your arrival in England?"

"Of course." She looked into Catherine's eyes, and the emotion she had fought so well slowly began to release. The two women embraced for a full minute before MaryAnne pushed back, took a deep breath, and, with one final glance to Catherine, took up the basket and climbed into the front seat of the car. Catherine shut the door behind her as David turned over the engine. MaryAnne looked once more to the home as the automobile pulled away.

✦

The depot bustled with the usual cacophony of an arriving train. The Los Angeles Limited had completed its Salt Lake City disembarkment, and the last of the Salt Lake passengers were in process of boarding. David transported the bulky luggage to the east platform, relinquishing them to a burly, black porter who examined MaryAnne's ticket, then carried the bags on board.

David scratched his head. "I do not know why I feel so apprehensive about your journey. I am not one for premonition."

"I feel this way every time you leave," MaryAnne said truthfully. "You are just not used to seeing me off."

"I am sure you are right."

A blast of steam whistled from the train's engine.

"You have everything?"

She nodded, then glanced anxiously around the harried depot. "I should board," she said. David pulled her in close, engaging her in a long, ardent kiss. Suddenly he drew back.

"What is the matter?"

MaryAnne turned away. Just then the train released a hiss of steam, followed by the conductor's warning shout that echoed through the depot.

"MaryAnne . . ."

"You worry too much about me. I will manage."

He pulled her to him again, placing his cheek against hers. "Come home soon."

MaryAnne took a deep breath, desperately fighting back the emotions and the man she wished to succumb to.

"Good-bye, David."

She walked briskly to the moving train, beckoned by a porter who clung to the rail between the cars and helped her board. David watched as the train departed the station. As he returned to his automobile, a peculiar thought flashed across his mind which he just as quickly brushed aside—for there was no reason to believe that he would never see his wife again.

◆

When David returned from MaryAnne's departure, he found Gibbs, his company clerk, standing in the threshold of his office.

"Congratulations," Gibbs announced, "we now qualify as the state's largest private charity."

David stepped past him to his desk, casually examining the documents that had appeared on it overnight. He spoke without looking up. "How bad is it?"

"Wages in January exceed company profit. When next quarter's orders decrease, we'll be overstaffed by twelve men." He walked to the front of David's desk and reclined in a leather wing chair. "We cannot support this many employees without selling company holdings." He waited for David to advance the obvious remedy, then, deciding it was not forthcoming, proceeded with it himself. "We cannot delay the inevitable any longer . . . it is time we start laying off."

"How does our net look?"

"Happily, gold stocks continue to climb. When you told me ten years ago to start taking payment in stock from the gold mines I thought you were just being charitable. They've gone from forty-eight dollars a share to more than six hundred. My only regret is that we didn't take more."

"Never trusted banks," David said laconically.

"Wisely, apparently."

David sat down at his desk and pushed aside the clutter from its surface. "Where will they go?"

"Who?"

"The employees you would have me lay off. Sharecropping? Panhandling? Suicide?"

"It's not your concern what happens to them."

"Whose is it?"

The retort stumped Gibbs.

"The Depression won't last forever. I don't want to lose a single employee if possible."

"Profits can't support them all."

"Then we'll tighten our belts."

"We already have."

"Then we'll tighten them more," David said. "Cut salaries across the board—including administration."

"You mean you and me."

"Implicitly."

"It won't solve all of our problems. A pay cut will be a hardship on all the workers. There are already factions forming within the company."

"What kind of factions?"

"There is a group that thinks the Negroes should all be laid off. I hear that some of these men are with the Ku Klux Klan."

The news, though of little surprise, was of great concern. Propelled by the tide of economic austerity, the resentment of "Negroes taking white men's jobs" had washed across the continent in a burgeoning wave, leaving in its wake a spell of lynchings—for a dead black man not only told no tales but left a vacancy in the job market as well. The swell had finally crashed down on his company's doorstep.

"The balloon dips and everyone starts looking for

ballast," David said caustically. "These are mean days."

"They will get meaner," Gibbs prophesied.

"Anything else we need to discuss?"

Gibbs stood, pushing himself up from his knees. "We could be profitable," he said as if the prospect had entirely eluded David. David grinned at his friend's tenacity. "What profiteth a man to gain the whole world and lose his soul . . ."

"I was not aware sainthood was one of our business objectives."

"It's not. I just prefer sleeping at night."

"At least someone can sleep," Gibbs said. Then, suddenly remembering, asked, ". . . the governor's Holiday Charity Ball at Saltair. It is still a few months away, but shall I RSVP for us?"

"I'll postal a contribution."

"I wasn't asking if you intended to contribute. Elaine and I hoped that you and MaryAnne would join us. If I might be presumptuous, it would be good for the two of you to dance."

"Dance?"

"People do it from time to time."

"It's been a lifetime."

"It is none of my affair, but with the hours and travel you impose on yourself, I cannot see how the two of you find the time to even see each other—let alone dance."

"I recall you once chiding me for not spending enough time at work."

"Things change."

David looked to the wall calendar and counted days. "I don't think MaryAnne will have returned yet from Britain. And you are right, Gibbs."

Gibbs was surprised at David's concession. "Really?"

"Yes. It is none of your affair."

Gibbs smiled in surrender as he walked out the door.

✦

Gibbs immediately informed the company of the pending pay cuts, and by late afternoon a small group of sullen-faced men congregated outside David's office. At David's behest, the men entered. There were nine men in all, staggered in height and width, their attire was worn and soiled from the mechanics they performed on the work floor below. David sat at his desk while Gibbs stood a few feet behind him, his hands clasped behind his back. Gibbs leered at the men, suspicious of their intentions.

"What may I do for you?" David asked.

The chosen mouthpiece of the delegation stepped forward, holding a felt fedora at his waist. He was a florid, balding man, a floor supervisor who oversaw the production of the iron-casted parts for ore cars, keeves, and kibbles.

"Mr. Parkin, the boys and I would like to speak our minds concerning the recent cut in wages."

Gibbs put his hands in his trouser pockets and leaned back against the window's perimeter, his demeanor perceptibly grown more vehement. Contrarily, David smiled, seeking to assuage the man's anxiety. "Please."

"We know things been slow of late and require a cutback—don't get us wrong, ain't a one of us complainin'. Fact I was just sayin' that most companies been through three or four pay cuts by now, wasn't I boys?" He nodded to the congregation who, on cue, bobbed and grunted in affirmation.

He hesitantly proceeded. ". . . But we thinkin' . . . rather than cause undue hardship . . . maybe the more decent thing be to just let the Negroes go. We knowed we could do just fine without 'em. Wouldn't slow production up. You can have our word on that."

Gibbs inhaled deeply, anticipating David's impassioned response. To his surprise, David merely reclined in his chair hearing the request with apparent interest.

"You are Mr. Boggs, am I correct?"

"Yes, sir. Judd Boggs."

"Mr. Boggs, how long have you been employed at my company?"

"Since I came to the valley. Goin' on nearly five years now."

"Before the Depression."

"Yes, sir."

"Do you feel that you have been treated fairly here?"

"Yes, sir. Been treated real good. Don't think many bossmen care as much to even ask such a question."

The men again bobbed and grunted in consensus.

"Five years. Are you aware that some of these Negroes you speak of have worked here for more than twenty years—a trifle longer than you. In fact a few of them are among my most productive workers."

"Didn't say they ain't good workers," he said unabashedly. "Just Negroes."

David raised a pen and began tapping it against the desk as he considered his response. His voice sounded weary. "It is not easy running a company. I am told by my advisor here that I should have already laid off a third of my workers—that all of my profits are being eaten up by wages of employees that do not have enough to do. What do you think of that?"

Judd clenched his hat. "You're right charitable, Mr. Parkin. Like I said, work been slow—Depression and all. That's why we thought maybe it'd be in your best interest to put out the Negroes."

"My best interest?" David's jaw tightened, the only indication of the emotion that brooded behind his controlled demeanor. He leaned forward across his desk. "Do you pretend to know my best interest, Mr. Boggs?"

The man's face twitched. "No, sir."

"You men are still working here at my expense

and by my grace and you come to me to ask if I won't fire your coworkers? How should I respond to that?"

"But . . . we talkin' about just the darkies," he stammered in clarification.

"Of course—they're only darkies. Darkies don't suffer, do they? Their children don't feel hunger pangs like yours do. They don't know fear. Don't worry about taking care of their own." He shook his head incredulously. "They are just darkies."

The man replied nothing, while a few, near the rear of the congregation, squirmed uncomfortably, convicted by their own consciences.

"Mr. Boggs, if you, or any of your esteemed colleagues, value your employment, then I suggest you return to it and never speak of this matter on my grounds or my time again. If you cannot endure working side by side with the Negroes perhaps you should try standing beside them in the breadlines because there's already more than enough of them there. Is that perfectly clear?"

"Yes, sir."

David's voice rose. "I am not just addressing Mr. Boggs."

"Yes, sir," the group replied in staggered and startled response.

"Then return to your work. You should consider yourself fortunate that I am more merciful than you."

The men turned on their heels and quickly dis-

appeared back into the cacophony of the work-
place.

An hour after the end of the workday, Gibbs poked
his head into David's office. David sat at his desk
studying several blue-ink plans that lay flat before
him. To one side of the table, an opened leather
valise had spilled its contents to the crowded surface.

"Eventful day," Gibbs said.

"It breaks the monotony, at least."

Gibbs leaned against the doorjamb. "I'm a clerk.
I like monotony."

David smiled without looking up from his task.

"Elaine and I are going out for some dinner.
Would you care to join us?"

"Thank you, but I think I'll stay and finish some
of these quotes."

"You'll be a bachelor for a while. Maybe next
week."

"I'll look forward to it. Give Elaine my love."

Gibbs gave David a mock salute and left him to
his drawings.

CHAPTER 4

The Silent
Parlor

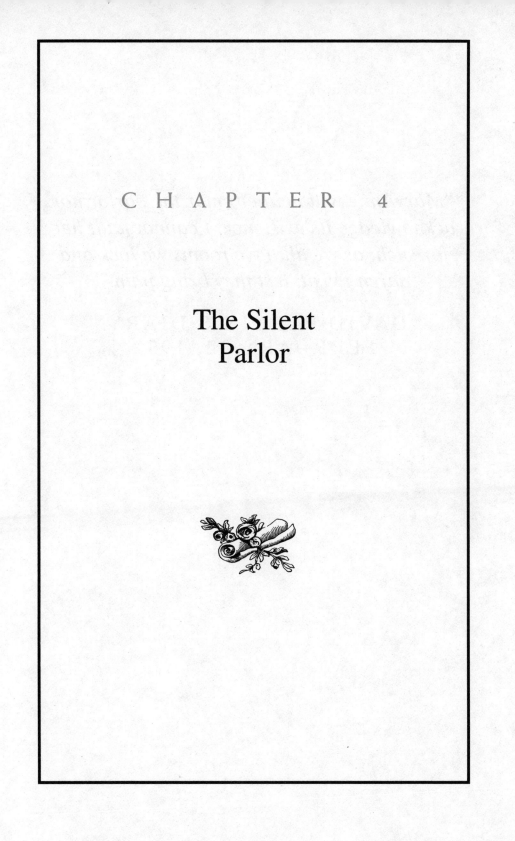

"MaryAnne will neither enter the parlor nor acknowledge its existence. I cannot fault her for such, as we all have rooms we lock and daren't visit, lest they bring pain."

DAVID PARKIN'S DIARY.
FEBRUARY 22, 1932

Amongst the Victorian architecture of the Salt Lake City Avenues, the Parkin mansion was an edifice of singular grandeur. It had originally been constructed as the residence of Salt Lake City's second mayor, the honorable Thomas Nash. Nash was a federally appointed easterner who viewed the city's inhabitants as cretins and simpletons, and brazenly used his position to advance his financial situation. When the mayor made vulgar advances on one of the city's venerable widows he was run out of town on a rail. Three days later, sixty miles north of the city, he was recognized by an inebriated relative of the widow and was shot outside an Ogden saloon and left for the city undertaker for a pauper's burial. It was an era of great pragmatism in western politics.

The disreputed mayor had spared little expense in the creation and furnishing of the mansion, garnishing the home with all the fineries the city had to offer, and many that it didn't, requiring great shipments from the mills and factories of the East and beyond the Atlantic. Each of its thirteen rooms was rendered with unique resplendence—consistent only in extravagance.

Inlaid parquetry floors were dressed with beautiful rugs and tapestries, English Victorian chenilles or Oriental weaves, matched in opulent competition with the ceilings, bedecked with exquisite, intricate stencil works and fixtures—chandeliers of crystal and bronze, from Strasbourg and Lancashire, hung from elaborately carved ceiling rosettes painted pastel and gilt.

The home's windows were crowned with stained-glass designs of fruit or seraphs, while the designs of the door panes and the humbler windows—florals and rococo flourishes—were etched in the blue-tint glass.

David Parkin had purchased the mansion in 1902 and was joined by MaryAnne, in matrimony and home, six years later. In 1913 the home had undergone extensive renovation as a result of the fire that had taken their daughter's life. Ironically, the room most affected by the tragedy had never been touched by flames. The second-floor parlor. It was in the parlor where, one day after the fire, Andrea had died. Its threshold had not been trespassed since.

✦

It was past one o'clock in the morning when David returned home. Though he was accustomed to working late, with MaryAnne's absence he felt even less impetus to return at any seemly hour. Catherine had retired long before, leaving the house dark.

Despite the late hour, David went to the drawing

room, switched on a single lamp, and poured himself a shot of brandy from a crystal decanter as he reclined into his Turkish armchair, propping his feet before him on a leather ottoman. It was then that he first noticed the envelope that Catherine, at MaryAnne's request, had left on the side table beside his chair. He recognized MaryAnne's script and seal, set down his drink, and took up the envelope. He could not recall the last time she had written him a letter, and he opened it with great curiosity.

✦

My beloved David,
No matter how I write, the words fall so cruel, I wish I could use them more sparingly. This is farewell, my love. I shall not return from London. I do not know anymore if my departure is right or wrong, I have reasoned until I can think no more—all I know is what I feel and what I can bear. Or cannot. I can no longer endure the pain of your alienation. Your love was my sun, David, and the walls you have built around your heart have deprived me of its warmth until my heart has wilted. My departure is only the final act of a separation that took place years ago and what we have prolonged has only mocked the beauty of what we once shared. It is with

heartbreak that I admit that our marriage died with our daughter.

I know that you love me—as I do you. This is what has given wings to my flight, for love is a traitorous emotion. Never once did you hold it against me that you were not Andrea's birth father, yet it is thrown back at you daily as you cannot give me more children and you blame yourself for losing our only. You did not lose our daughter, David. Andrea's death was caused by the cruel actions of evil men. You were nothing but courageous and compassionate. Shall we not stand up to evil because it threatens our personal situation? If we do not, evil will always prevail. You taught me this and although you may know that you did the right thing, you do not believe it. There is a difference, and in that difference I have lost my husband. I cannot change your heart, I can only break the cycle of our pain.

Forgive me for my weakness—for bidding farewell in ink, not words. I could not face you. I was afraid that you would implore me to stay and I would not be able to resist. How could I deny the man I cherish more than all? I once gave you my life, David, but I had never imagined that I would steal away yours. I give it back to you. I beg you to not pursue me. Go and be free.

You are forever in my heart.

MARY

✦

David gaped at the writing as if awaiting the explanation to a vicious hoax—but the words held no hope of such blessed cruelty. As its truth settled, his mind reeled in a thousand thoughts and directions, all equally horrible. It was as if the great wall of protection with which he had surrounded his heart had been pierced, and his vulnerable heart, rendered all the more defenseless from years of shelter, felt that it would burst. He wanted to run to her, to stop her, to scream back the train that carried her away.

He grabbed the decanter and drank directly from it. The brandy burned his throat. He read the letter again, half hoping for some alteration of its message—some line that he may have overlooked—some reprieve from the pain that spread throughout his body, faster than the liquor that numbed it. He began to cry, wiping his tears with the same hand that held the bottle, following each bout with another drink until the bottle was nearly half drained.

Clutching the note and bottle in one hand, he staggered out of the room, inexplicably drawn up the darkened staircase. At the door of the upstairs parlor he extracted a skeleton passkey from his breast pocket, fumbled with the instrument, then, for the first time since their daughter's death, opened the door. He reached inside and switched on a lamp. It was as if he had stepped back into the past and the flood of memory that washed over him drew his thoughts from his pain. The room was a time capsule, perfectly preserved from twenty years previous—each article, once ardently sought and admired, now carried greater meaning because of its absence from his life.

The day Andrea had died in the parlor, the room had been pronounced dead and as if by mutual assent, life inside the room ground to a halt. The room's clocks fulfilled their obligations until springs unwound and pendulums faltered, wearing on their spandreled faces the hour of their death. Even the greater clockwork of the cosmos had been kept at bay behind drapes which grew moth-eaten and faded through time. Dust had settled in a singular sheet on the room in a grey, batting-like shroud. Spiders had woven the room in their silk tapestries as intricate as those wrought from Indian looms that lay on its floor.

In the corner of the room was the tiny bed. Its sheets remained in the same throw as when they had been peeled back and their daughter's lifeless body was carried out. David quickly looked past it to the far wall, where towered the grandfather's clock that he had given MaryAnne on their wedding night—and stopped at the moment of their daughter's death. He had given MaryAnne the prized clock as a symbol of the meaning she had brought to his life. Now it stood motionless. He threateningly raised the decanter to its glass-enclosed face, then turned and hurled the bottle against the opposite wall where it exploded into crystal shards. He leaned back against the wall next to the clock and slumped down until he rested on the floor, his knees pulled up to his chest.

The parlor lay only a few doors from Catherine's room, and she had hurried from her quarters, awakened by the crash. Astonished to find light coming from the parlor, she rushed to its threshold. She gasped when she found David on the floor against its far wall. The stench of alcohol wafted through the room. He looked up at her, his eyes lifeless, his face streaked with tears. Their eyes met. In all her years in his service she had never seen him drunk, and she awaited his actions with fearful anticipation. David was the first to speak, his voice heavy with emotion.

"MaryAnne never came in here. There were too many memories . . ."

"David. What has happened?"

He shook his head, as if unwilling to accept the news he bore. "She's not coming back," he cried incredulously. "MaryAnne's not coming back."

Catherine took two steps into the room. "Not coming back?"

With a trembling hand he offered the letter to her. Catherine walked to him and took the parchment.

"Dear Lord," she exclaimed, biting down on her lower lip.

David began to sob, burying his face into his knees. Catherine, equally fraught, knelt down by his side. He looked up at her. His face suddenly flashed to rage. "Did you know about this? About her plans to leave me?!"

"David!"

"Did you know?!" he demanded.

Her body, as well as her voice, began to tremble. "David, you are frightening me."

His harsh voice faltered, sublimating to pleading sobs ". . . did you know?"

Catherine struggled to speak, her own voice surrendering to emotion as well. "Of course I didn't know," she cried. "Oh, Mary, what have you done?"

David again began to cry and Catherine put her arms around him, maternally pulling his head into her breast. When his sobbing subsided he looked up into her eyes. "I have loved three women in my life, Catherine. And I have lost them all . . ."

Catherine brushed back a tear from her own cheek.

". . . But MaryAnne's abandonment is the only one I deserved."

✦

Morning found David in the sanctuary of his den recording his thoughts in his diary. The habit of his journal writing had a therapeutic effect, not that he had consciously determined this, rather, it was simply a natural act, as one might seek shelter from a storm. His head and heart ached from the previous night and his pen wandered slowly across the page.

✦

"I feel so lost.

No. To be lost is to not know where one is—and I am all too sure. I am alone. My heart, my love, has been torn from me and I am consumed by the pain of that loss.

Yet I feel MaryAnne around me as keenly as before. Maybe more so. For I see her absence in all the evidences of the home that she left behind.

I am a fool. What selfishness so blinded my heart that I could not see that she still required its nourishment?

My pen rambles with more foolishness. I mourn what I am missing and the pain that pierces my heart—not hers. This is the paradox that keeps MaryAnne from my reach—for to go after her, for my heart's sake, is to be unworthy of her. Could it be that to truly love a thing is not to desire it, but to desire happiness for it? If so, I cannot have her back, to relieve my heart at the expense of hers. If I truly love her.

And I do love her. More than my own life I love her.

I can only hope that she might return. Yet hope is oftentimes the cruelest of virtues.

How did I come to such a dark place? I don't know where my road now leads but I fear the shadowlands that lie ahead. But it is not the darkness of the path I fear. Just the loneliness of the trail."

DAVID PARKIN'S DIARY. OCTOBER 21, 1933

CHAPTER 5

Victoria's
Introduction

"Even as I withheld my love from MaryAnne, she had never stopped filling me with hers. I had never supposed how cold my world would be without her warmth."

DAVID PARKIN'S DIARY.
NOVEMBER 2, 1933

It was nearly a fortnight before David returned to the office, an occurrence which proved to be a vicarious act mostly, for he spent the better part of the morning staring out the window of his second-story office, as oblivious to the activity of his company as he was to the street's activity which he blindly observed. Around noontime Gibbs entered his office. David did not greet him. Gibbs shut the door and walked to his side. "I am glad that you are returned, David."

"How have things been in my absence?"

"The month's orders have not declined as much as I had anticipated, so with the pay cuts we may actually come out ahead. The men you chastised have prudently taken your counsel and have not broached the Negro issue again. That is what I am told by those on the floor." Gibbs looked at David empathetically. He knew that he had lost him even before he had finished his response. "Go after her, David."

David raked a hand back through his hair. "I can't, Gibbs. I would carry her back in chains if I knew that it could be different . . ." His voice fell like the second refrain of an echo. ". . . If I could be different. I can't promise that. I don't even know where to start." He bowed his head. "She has buried me, Gibbs. My love has buried me. The dead should stay put."

For many years, Gibbs had counseled David on all his affairs, from the daily running of his plant to the rituals of courtship. He had never before felt so inadequate. He put his hand on David's back. "If anyone ever belonged together it was the two of you. It just doesn't seem right. If there is anything that I can do . . ."

"I would like for you to arrange with her brother a financial settlement. I want her to live in the manner to which she is accustomed." He added, ". . . at least financially."

"I will wire him immediately."

At that moment, David's secretary peered through his door. "Mr. Parkin, Mrs. Piper is outside. She insists on seeing you."

David grimaced. "Word travels."

"I'll get rid of her," Gibbs said.

"No, I might as well see her. At least someone will derive joy from my misfortune."

Gibbs frowned as he left the room, passing on his exit Victoria Piper, a local socialite and flagship of the city's haute monde. She strut-waddled into the office, momentarily eclipsing the light from the doorway with her ever-widening girth.

"I will be brief, David. I know that you do not wish to speak with me."

David made no effort to deny the allegation. She sat down opposite his desk.

"Honestly, I do not know why you treat me so petulantly. I have only your best interests at heart."

David responded to the assertion with as cordial a voice as he could intone. "And what interests of mine do you have in your heart today?"

She ignored his sarcasm. "I am the chairwoman of the governor's charity ball this Christmas. Will you and MaryAnne be attending?"

"MaryAnne will not be available."

"So I had heard," she said with particular relish. "I am sorry that she is indisposed."

David glowered.

Victoria said thoughtfully, "I think you should meet my niece, David. She is arriving from Chicago next Thursday for my cousin Lucy's bridal shower and will be staying with me through the holidays."

"You have never felt the inclination to acquaint me with your kin before now. Why would I want to meet your niece?"

Victoria smiled benignly. "Oh, David. All men want to meet my niece."

Her intent infuriated him.

"I am married, Victoria."

"Yes, I was there," Victoria replied with the banal drawl she usually reserved for bad theater. "And how is that marriage, David?"

David bit back his anger and turned to his work,

bending over the stacks of carbon invoices that had piled up in his absence. "I am not interested."

Victoria was more amused by his response than dissuaded. She smiled easily as she stood to leave. "Oh, you will be, David. You will be."

CHAPTER 6

The Letter
Revealed

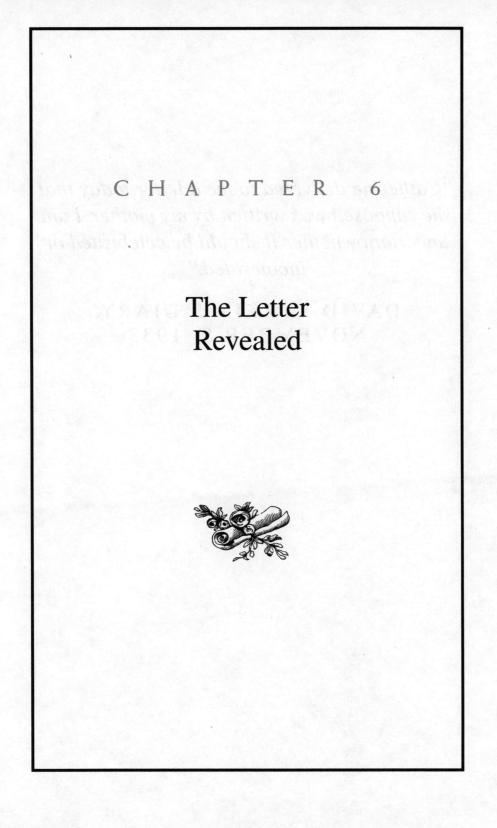

"Catherine delivered to me a letter today that she supposed was written by my mother. I am uncertain whether it should be celebrated or incinerated."

DAVID PARKIN'S DIARY.
NOVEMBER 9, 1933

In the quiet waning of a Sunday, Catherine entered the drawing room bearing a sterling tea service, a large, pear-shaped server bedecked by two, gold-rimmed cups with pink florals baked into their porcelain enamel. David sat motionless, embraced in the wide, tapestry cushions of his Turkish chair, as a string ensemble of the *Messiah* from the *Ford Sunday Evening Hour* filled the room. The radio was positioned just an arm's length from his side—an RCA cabinet with cathedral carvings on the face of the polished walnut console. David stared blankly into the fireplace at the orange-red embers from which clung the ebbing flames. The drapes had been drawn, and near the doorway a single lamp with an opaque, leather shade vaguely lit the room. Catherine pushed the door shut behind herself.

"I brought you some tea."

David looked over, noticing her entrance for the first time. "Thank you, Catherine," he said softly. He reached over and switched off the radio, which silenced with a death rattle of static. "Would you join me?"

"I would love to." She set the service on the parquet veneer of the lamp table, poured a cup to the brim, handed it to David, then turned and did the same for herself. She sat sideways on the ottoman before him.

"How is business?"

"Like trying to paddle a schooner up a dry riverbed."

Catherine smiled. "It is that bad?"

"I am afraid so. This drought has everyone on such edge. If we get through this without a lynching it will be a miracle."

Catherine's voice turned serious. "Is that what is troubling you?"

David sipped his tea, then sat back into the chair looking thoughtful. "No. Actually, I was thinking about my father."

Catherine cocked her head. "It has been many years since you have spoken of your father."

"He was a good man. And he was wise. I wish he was still around."

Catherine nodded sympathetically.

"You know, he never once complained about my mother leaving us. Even after I had grown. I guess maybe he thought it was inevitable. I never saw it—with her or MaryAnne."

"You can't compare MaryAnne with your mother."

"I know that it's different, but it feels the same." He gazed blankly at his cup while his thoughts coalesced. "I remember the morning that my mother left. I was curled up in the hallway as she packed her trunks. When she came out with her cases I asked her where she was going. She said Nevada

City. It was true, in part. The train out of California rode through Nevada City."

An air pocket exploded in the nearly depleted log in the fireplace, and Catherine looked to see if any sparks had escaped the hearth.

"I didn't want to believe that she was gone. Even after my father told me that she wasn't coming back, I didn't believe him. I held on to her for nearly a year—until Christmas. I am doing the same with MaryAnne. Just trying to hold on."

"It is only natural," Catherine said gently.

"My mother had this playbill on the wall of her bedroom—the only art in the house. It was a picture of a woman surrounded by black, demonic, winged creatures. It terrified me. When I realized that my mother wasn't coming back, I connected those demons with her disappearance and tore up the poster and threw dirt on it." David bowed his head and his voice grew in emotion. "There are just things that I don't understand. You know I would have given anything to have my Andrea back. Anything."

"Of course you would have . . ."

"Then how is it that my mother abandoned me? I wasn't taken from her, she gave me up. She willingly gave me up." His voice rose with indignation. "How could she do that?"

The question was as unanswerable to Catherine as it was to him, though she wondered for an instant if he truly spoke of his mother or Mary-Anne.

"It is a ghost that has haunted me my whole life. It was chased away for a season by Andrea, but it has returned. It would make all the difference in my life if I could only ask my mother why."

"If you had the chance you would talk to her?"

"If I had the chance I would ask her questions until every demon had left my soul." David rested his head in his palm. "I don't even know if she is still alive."

Catherine silently contemplated his words then set her china teacup next to the caddy. "David, I need to share something with you."

David looked up as she stood.

"I must retrieve it from my quarters."

She left the room, returning a few moments later with a wrinkled envelope. The parcel filled him with foreboding.

"Is it from Mary?"

"MaryAnne gave it to me before she left. But she didn't write it." She held out to him the envelope. The wrinkled paper bore the water-stains of the snow that had once blanketed it and run its ink. The rose seal was unfamiliar to him. He removed its contents.

✦

Dearest Child,
That I did not know you, my loss is greatest.
Forgive me for the pain I have brought to those
who love you.

*So gladly would I trade my sad life for your
realm.*
Angel, watch over this little one.

⁛

"Where did you get this?"

"MaryAnne found it at Andrea's grave. She didn't
want you to see it."

"Why?"

"She thought it would bring you pain." Catherine
hesitated. ". . . She feared that it was left by your
mother."

"My mother?" David returned his gaze to the letter. Suddenly he set his cup on the tray, stood, and
walked from the room. When Catherine caught up
to him, he was standing on the middle rung of an
oak book ladder facing a rosewood bookshelf that
climbed to the ceiling. He was searching amidst a
row of books six shelves above the library's parquet floor. Books of his own writing—his journals.

David extracted one of several leather-bound di-
aries and brought it to a mahogany, Queen Anne
writing desk. He leafed through its pages until discovering the insert he searched for—a brittle,
folded parchment, no larger than his hand—folded
once, then pressed flat between the pages. It was
the penned regret he had received thirty-six years
previous from his mother. He carefully lifted it

from the book, unfolded it, and pressed it flat against the desk's surface, to the side of the note Catherine had delivered minutes earlier. Though it had been pressed in the book for more than three decades, it still showed evidence of David's first reaction to its message when he crumpled and threw it to the floor. He had retrieved the note a day later, preserving it in his journal.

✦

Dear David,
Such grand tidings I share. While awaiting your arrival in Salt Lake City, I met, by wonderful fate, a man from the Chicago theatre—a producer no less! I am returning tomorrow morning to Chicago to begin production of Bohemia, *where I shall play the role of Mimi. I shall send for you when the time is better.*

YOUR MOTHER,
ROSE

✦

Even now the note evoked pain. Pushing emotion aside, David meticulously scrutinized the documents, comparing the calligraphy letter by letter. There was a marked similarity in the penmanship of the two letters, though the scrawl of the more recent correspondence seemed frail and less disciplined.

David pointed out to Catherine the similarities.

"Note this letter . . . and here." His index finger rested on the page as his voice rose in excitement. "The scroll is nearly identical. But how would my mother know of Andrea? Or the angel?"

"It was in the papers—she could have learned of it. Who else could have left such a letter?"

"Why would she have come all this way and not come to see me?"

Catherine considered the question. "Perhaps she came to see but not to be seen. After all she has done to you she could hardly expect to be welcomed with open arms."

"No," David said almost to himself as he slowly turned back towards the letters. "She would not expect it." He slid the letters together and put them back between the pages of the journal. "Could you check with the local hotels to see if Rose King has registered with any of them in the last month."

"King?"

"It is my mother's maiden name."

The passion behind his request pleased her. "Of course. I will get right to it."

CHAPTER 7

Dierdre

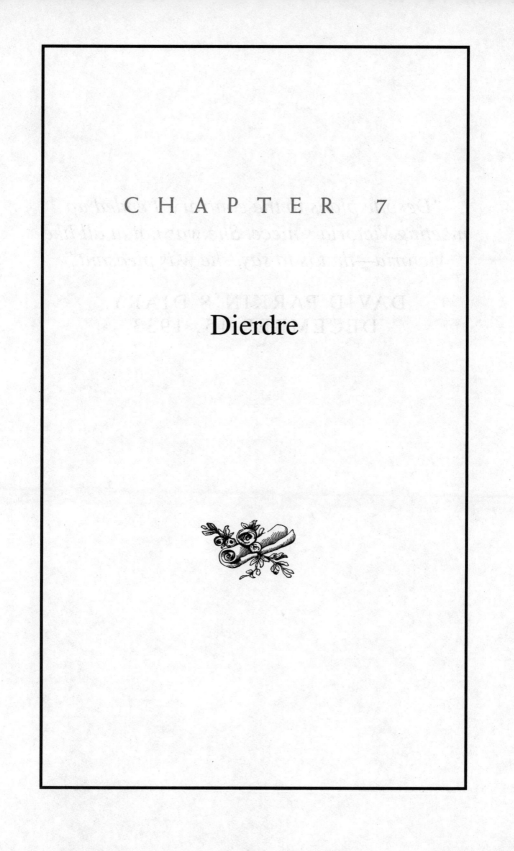

"Despite plans to the contrary, I ended up meeting Victoria's niece. She was not at all like Victoria—that is to say, she was pleasant."

DAVID PARKIN'S DIARY.
DECEMBER 15, 1933

The Saltair resort, erected on the salt-caked shores of the Great Salt Lake, was the pride of the great state of Utah and an oasis to some of the world's most popular bands and celebrities. Even Charles Lindbergh, on transcontinental tour with the craft that had carried him to celebrity, could not resist a dip in both the lake and its ballroom.

The last time David had been to Saltair was before the fire of twenty-five that had nearly burned the resort to the ground, and he only knew of the park's reconstruction from the local tabloids. Evidence of that fire still remained as an occasional charred wall or column lay concealed behind potted palms or fabric screens. The resort's main pavilion, a behemoth stucco-finished structure, was topped with Moorish domes, painted in vivid Mediterranean colors and patterns, purveying the romance of a story from the *Arabian Nights*. The ballroom, billed as the largest of its kind in the world, was elliptical in construction, its ceiling rising sixty feet above sprung floors of polished maple.

This evening, large painted banners proclaiming the holiday gala hung above each of the room's four keyhole archways, two of which exited to the planked boardwalk that extended four hundred feet out over the lake, a necessity for the resort's bathers as the capricious lake rose and fell with maddening uncertainty.

The evening's philanthropists paraded the pavilion floor in dance or strut, dressed in the masquerades of the affluent: black, wool tuxedos with long tails, spats, and silk top hats, and the more gracious sex in exquisite gowns of chiffon and silk with the high-necked décolletage the times demanded. There were few such socials in Salt Lake City, and when they came, those in attendance adorned themselves with the unabashed garishness of a Christmas tree.

Jerry Kirkham and the Saltair orchestra had just completed their sixth tune of the evening to the ardent reception of the dancers and lesser reaction by David who stood next to Gibbs, sipping white wine from a stemmed crystal wineglass, viewing the evening's proceedings with the dispassion of a spectator of the ballet. David had not participated in any social activity since MaryAnne's departure, and Gibbs, worried about David's increasing reclusiveness, had relentlessly insisted that he attend the event. When Gibbs's girl, Elaine, and Catherine joined in the campaign as well, David acquiesced, deciding it easier to go than to resist their entreatments.

Elaine emerged from the crowd, took Gibbs's hand, and pulled him towards the floor.

"C'mon, honey."

"Dancing is imminent," Gibbs said. "Take my drink, David?"

David took the glass with his own and walked to a nearby table and set them both down, then returned to his place at the edge of the human perimeter that marked the floor. As he followed their pirouette, his eye was suddenly attracted to a young woman, who, standing alone, likewise watched the dancers moving in sway to the brass tones of the band. She was arrestingly beautiful—as attractive as she was unique from those around her in both fashion and demeanor. She wore a tight-waisted dress of crepe de chine with a low waist-line and scandalously high hemline. Her hair was deep brunette, styled in a pageboy bob, slightly longer than permitted by the understated vogue of the austere decade. Her hat, a peach cloche, raked back to frame a facial structure of exquisite composition and further complemented her cream complexion. She smiled contentedly as she moved to the tune, fondling the pearls that encircled her neck.

Elaine and Gibbs suddenly reappeared next to him.

"Why don't you take a spin?" Gibbs shouted. "It will do you good."

"Yes," Elaine agreed, abruptly releasing her partner. "I would like a dance."

"You don't know what you are asking," David said. He obligingly took her hand and moved out to the crowded floor.

After a few steps David asked, "Is this why it is called a charity ball?"

"Oh, David. We love you."

". . . and pity me?"

Elaine smiled. "A little."

They had circled the floor just once when Gibbs tapped David's shoulder.

"I don't expect David and I will win the dance cup," Elaine announced.

"Ah," Gibbs replied, "but David is handsome and rich, which, in most decks, will beat a two-step. Precisely why I must cut back in."

"How sweet," Elaine cried, relinquishing David's hand for her lover's. "My man is jealous."

They immediately resumed their promenade. As David stepped back from the floor, he noticed that the young lady who had caught his eye was gone. He walked to a crystal punch bowl, ladled himself another drink, then stepped aside to resume his role as spectator. A petite, lace-gloved hand gently touched his sleeve.

"Would you care to dance?"

The question had been asked in a pleasant feminine voice with a hint of southern accent, and David turned to see the young woman he had noticed across the floor standing beside him.

"Dance?" she repeated. The woman gazed on him with piercing peacock blue eyes, nearly as lustrous as the bird's feathers. She smiled confidently. "I am sorry. I probably seem a bit forward."

"No, I just didn't expect to be dancing tonight."

"That is usually why one comes to a ball."

"Usually."

"Well," she said, the word drawn out for aesthetic effect, "as long as you are here . . ."

David smiled. "Why not." He abandoned his drink on a banister, took her arm, and led her to the floor, joining the dancers who gracefully spun to the Champagne Waltz.

"I have already been told tonight that I am not much of a dancer."

"You are doing fine," she said kindly. "I bet you are wicked with the Charleston."

"If wicked implies murderous, I am sure you are right."

The woman laughed and David smiled, worrying more about his step and marveling at hers. There was a simple grace to her motion—a carelessness free of the decade's burden.

"Are you new to the valley?"

"You mean Salt Lake City? No, my home is in Chicago. I am here just for a few weeks visiting with my aunt."

"Your aunt?"

"Yes, I came for a wedding."

David suddenly realized who she was. "You are Victoria's niece."

"You know Aunt Victoria?"

"She told me of your arrival," David replied. He glanced around the crowded room, suspect that Victoria had put the young woman up to the proposal. "Where is your aunt now?"

Dierdre followed his glance, then looked up into his face, her eyes sparkling with her offense. "It took some doing, but I lost her."

David chuckled at her candor. "Now why would you run out on your aunt?" he asked, perfectly willing to offer a hundred reasons himself.

"Tonight, she is a little too gregarious for my taste—that and her incessant nagging about coupling me with some man whose wife has just deserted him. Apparently he is rich, handsome, and pining—'a perfect combination,'" she said, mimicking her aunt's enunciation. "I told her that maybe the man's wife knows something that she doesn't." She read David's expression. "Oh, dear. He is not a friend of yours?"

David stopped dancing. "I believe your aunt was referring to me."

Dierdre flushed a deep crimson. "I am so embarrassed." She released his hand to go, but David took it up again. "I don't offend easily. And you are right. My wife does know something about me that Victoria doesn't."

They continued their promenade, the silence dragging on in agonizing minutes, with Dierdre turning away each time he ventured to look into her face. When the waltz concluded, she hastily thanked him and turned to leave.

"Just a moment," David said firmly.

She paused, awaiting a deserved rebuke.

"I hate to end a dance with the wrong step as much as I hate starting it with one." He grinned.

"Though I realize, with my dancing, it is hard to tell the difference."

She smiled.

". . . besides, I was cheated of a whole dance. It may be my only of the night."

The band's silent lull gave way to the opening refrain of the next song, "Two Cigarettes in the Dark."

She gently replied, "Then perhaps another dance would be in order."

David took her hand, and she returned hers to his shoulder and back. David tried to ease her discomfort with conversation.

"What do you think of our city?"

Her voice fell humbly, still reeling from the pain of her faux pas. "Quaint, but lovely. The moon on the lake is beautiful tonight."

"Have you taken a plunge?"

One corner of her mouth rose in a crooked smile. "Is this a threat?"

David grinned. "The Great Salt Lake is an oddity. Its concentration of salt is more than ten times that of the ocean. It is almost impossible to sink."

"No wonder my aunt finds this resort of such great amusement." Her mouth bent in an impish grin. "Though I am certain that she would be difficult to sink no matter the liquid."

At this David laughed loudly along with Dierdre who, pleased that she had made such an impression, momentarily forgot her earlier gaffe. As the dance progressed, she pressed her body, rich in the perfume of youth and femininity, tightly against his. She lay her head against his shoulder, and David began to feel emotions rise up inside not felt since he first met MaryAnne. When the band concluded the number, she made no effort to start from her position. David slowly began to draw away. At his movement, she stepped back.

"I hope I did not step on you too many times," David said.

"An occasional trampling keeps one alert," she jested. Her voice turned more sincere. "I am still very embarrassed by what I said. Sometimes I think I was born with a silver foot in my mouth."

"It is already forgotten."

"My aunt was right about you being very handsome. She failed to tell me that you are also very nice."

Their eyes met, and there was a discernible and mutual spark of attraction. David felt confused by the flux of emotions that suddenly overwhelmed him.

"Are you always so forthright?"

"Yes." Her face relaxed into an easy smile. "Well, almost always."

The noise and motion of the burgeoning crowd vanished into the moment's enchantment. Just then, Victoria stepped towards them, attired in a gaudy, flowing gown, layered in excessive yards of cream-colored fabric—flesh and cloth restrained by an overworked gold chenille sash. Her garb was outdone only by the wide grin on her overly rouged face.

"There you are, Dierdre," she blared, her arms outspread in lavish greeting. She said to David, "I should have suspected that you would be involved with my niece's abduction."

Dierdre rolled her eyes.

"I have been regaling the governor with your anecdotes, and he insists upon meeting you." She turned again to David. "He is waiting . . ."

Dierdre smiled shyly. "It was a pleasure making your acquaintance, David."

"Likewise," he replied clumsily.

Victoria observed David's awkwardness and smiled. She had anticipated this moment for the better part of the month and received his reaction with great satisfaction. David and Dierdre's chance encounter could not have gone better if she had orchestrated it herself. Dierdre offered David her hand. "Will I have the pleasure of seeing you again?"

"Of course you will, my dear," Victoria interjected, "I will see to it."

"Good night, David," she said softly.

"Good night," he returned.

"And good night to you, David," Victoria said with a triumphant smile, then took her niece by the arm and whisked her away to her next social imperative.

CHAPTER 8

The Morning
After

"A broken heart is always looking for a mend."

DAVID PARKIN'S DIARY.
DECEMBER 15, 1933

"You were out late last night," Catherine observed as she stretched a pale, linen shirt over a fabric-sheathed clothes board. She dipped her hand in a bowl of water and sprinkled it over the material's surface. To her side, an iron poised vertically on its wide hips. David sat at the kitchen table, dressed for the day except for the absence of shirt and tie, his suspenders crossing his bare torso.

"I believe Elaine mistook the affair for a dance marathon. I ended up waiting alone out on the beach. There is something about a body of water that stirs the mind."

"It's been years since I have been to Saltair," Catherine reminisced. "Or cut a rug." She pushed the iron across the shirt. "Did you dance?"

"I would never be convicted of it."

"With whom did you dance?"

"Once with Elaine."

With her closed hand she flattened down the shirt's collar. "Anyone else?"

David smiled at her surreptitiously.

"I was not prying. I was only curious."

"Pray tell the difference."

Catherine shook her head. "Since you are obviously uncomfortable with the question, I will withdraw it."

"I danced with Victoria's niece."

Catherine pretended to be disinterested. "I did not know she had a niece in the area."

"She doesn't. Dierdre is from Chicago."

"Dierdre." Catherine repeated the name slowly, committing it to memory. "Is she anything like her aunt?"

David sipped his coffee as if he hadn't heard the question, and Catherine knew when to change the topic.

"You haven't mentioned the Christmas pine. Don't you like it?"

"I'm sorry. I haven't felt festive of late. It's beautiful. Are the ornaments new?"

"No." She smiled. "Same ones we've used for the last ten years." Her voice softened. ". . . About Christmas. My aunt in Park City has invited me up for Christmas dinner. I have yet to accept." She studied David's reaction.

"Why not?"

"I thought maybe you would join us."

"I appreciate your sympathy, Catherine. But I will be fine. It will be nice for you to spend some time with your family. It's been a long while since you spent Christmas with family."

"What about you?"

"Gibbs and Elaine have invited me to dine with them on Christmas Eve. That is about all the festivities I'm up to."

She went back to her ironing. "Then I will go,"

she said reticently. She lifted his shirt. "I am sorry that you have nothing to wear. Yesterday was ironing day, and I was out checking on the hotels you asked me to."

"I am in no particular hurry this morning. How did your search go?"

"The hotels weren't very helpful. Only two of them would check back to last month's registers. None of them show a Rosalyn King, or Parkin, as a guest. If she was in town, she isn't anymore."

David's brow furrowed. "I wonder if she has returned to Chicago?"

"If she didn't plan on seeing you I see no reason she would stay."

"Did you, perchance, visit with the sexton? I am told that he never leaves the cemetery. He might have noticed someone at the angel."

Catherine brought him the freshly pressed shirt, then returned to her bloated laundry basket. "I had not considered that. I would be happy to speak with him."

"Perhaps on your way back from Lawrence's this morning."

Catherine draped a pleated skirt across the board. "Speaking of Lawrence, I am worried about him. He is acting very peculiar."

"I saw him only four days ago. He was in reasonably high spirits."

"When I visited him yesterday, he had not eaten

any of his food from the day before. I asked him why, and he replied rather sharply that he did not care to discuss it."

"Lawrence said that?"

"It is peculiar."

"Did he say anything else?"

"He kept talking about dying."

"That is standard fare. He has talked of dying for the last decade."

"It is different now. It is more than conversation. He said something about wanting to be buried next to a woman named Margaret. In fact, he mentioned her several times. Do you know who she is?"

"Margaret? He has never spoken of her to me. Any woman for that matter." He set down his empty cup. "I will drop by Lawrence's tonight, I am due a visit." His voice softened as if either embarrassed by the question he asked or the response he feared. "Have you heard from MaryAnne?"

"No. Not yet."

He nodded gently, walked to the doorway, then stopped. ". . . Dierdre is nothing like her aunt."

✦

Victoria and Dierdre settled for brunch in high-backed wicker chairs in the sunroom of the Piper mansion, surrounded by the maids and butlers who were decking the home in the gold and silver tinsel of holiday attire. A centerpiece of pine cones and mistletoe adorned the table they sat at. Victoria's garish laughter resounded throughout the wing as the two women ruminated on the previous evening's escapades.

"So, now that you have met the man, what do you think of our Mr. Parkin?"

"I find him charming." A smile of amusement curled her lips. "He seems unsure of himself around women. It is a trait I am especially fond of in men."

Victoria chortled. "Why do I not find that surprising?"

Dierdre asked seriously, "Do you suppose I was too forward?"

"Forward is what forward does," Victoria proffered. "Truthfully, I think David was quite taken with you. He was behaving so peculiarly." She raised a colorful, long-stemmed glass to her lips.

Dierdre smiled. "I like his peculiar. There is a certain . . . virility."

"Perhaps you mean vulgarity. It is a standard of the nouveau riche." Victoria read the displeasure on Dierdre's face and quickly repented. "But he does have a certain charm."

"I find him *very* charming," Dierdre asserted in defiance of her aunt's observations. "And very handsome."

"He is that. And clever. While other men lost their fortunes in the crash, he quadrupled his. You should witness the plebeians lined up outside his company each morning scavenging for work. I have the misfortune of having to pass it daily on way to the club. It is so odious."

Dierdre ignored the overt callousness of her aunt's remarks. "What of his wife? Has she granted him a divorce?"

"I don't believe so."

"Does he still love her?"

"He seems devoted to her, though I suspected fissures in the union even before her flight. Men hide behind their employment when the company at home becomes disagreeable, and David travels unceasingly. I wonder that he ever goes home." She rested her glass on a squat, wicker table and pointed a stout finger at her niece. "Someone would be doing him a service to free him of such drudgery."

"You believe then that his marriage is imperiled?"

Victoria again broke into ostentatious laughter. "My dear, all marriages are imperiled. That is precisely why one must marry right. To ensure a comfortable solitude."

"You *are* dreary today."

"And you are romantic," Victoria retorted. "Though I will not seek to dissuade you from your illusions. They will shatter soon enough. And if I am dreary, it is this blasted climate. I do not know why I stay in this miserable desert." She held out a corpulent wrist. "Look how dry my skin is. I would have fled east decades ago had I not been so lazy." At this she yawned.

"Aunt, you will never leave Salt Lake City. Utah society would collapse without a puppeteer of your dexterity."

Victoria beamed.

"Do you suppose that David will call on me?"

"I would think so, but who could know? I have long stopped trying to foretell the man's ways."

"I hope that he does," Dierdre said wistfully. She held up a sprig of mistletoe and smiled. "I hope that he visits on Christmas Eve." She sat back in her chair and picked at a plate of winter melon and pears, momentarily abdicating all conversation to the servants in the outer corridors.

C H A P T E R 9

A Glass
Sliver

"I stopped by Lawrence's this evening and, in the course of our visit, he hinted at something I had never before imagined—that he had once been married. It is a peculiar thing to believe that you know someone intimately only to find that you really do not. It is like finishing a book only to discover that you have missed several key chapters."

DAVID PARKIN'S DIARY.
DECEMBER 17, 1933

As dusk blanketed the city in its tenebrous shadow, David drove his Packard down the steep and darkened alleyway of the now vacant cannery building and turned off the concrete path at the dirt front entryway of Lawrence's shanty. He clutched a paper sack from the seat beside him, stepped from the car, then rapped on Lawrence's door with his free hand.

"Come in, David."

David slowly opened the door. Except for the amber radiance of the coal fire, obscured beneath the thick grate of the potbelly stove, the room was pitch black—of little consequence to a blind man.

"One of these times I will change my knock."

"Ain't your knock, it's your automobile's. If I still had my eyes I'd get under your hood."

"I have been meaning to get to it," David replied. "Maybe now with MaryAnne gone." It was a foolish excuse, and he felt foolish for thinking it. David took up a box of matches and lit the charred wick of the kerosene army lantern that hung from the rafter above the cot, taking mental note of its diminishing store of fuel. The pungent smell of sulphur wafted throughout the chamber. David squatted to open the stove's grate and fed the waning fire from a scuttle of coal. He reached over to an adjacent washbasin, then rose, lifting with him two shot glasses. He sat down to the table across from his friend.

"I brought you a Christmas present." He pushed an unwrapped box his way.

Lawrence felt the box, lifted its lid, and felt the cast image inside. "It's an angel. Is it brass?"

"It is sterling silver. Merry Christmas, my friend."

"Thank you, David."

He pulled the bottle from his bag. "And I brought some scotch."

"What's the occasion?"

"None's as good as any." David poured the first glass and pushed it across the table to Lawrence, who followed its motion by sound. Lawrence lifted the glass but did not drink.

"'Bout what hour it gettin' to be?"

It was an odd question to hear from Lawrence, and David glanced around the room at the gathered clocks. For the first time in thirty years they were silent.

"Around nine. Maybe ten minutes past." His forehead condensed. "Catherine says you haven't been eating."

"Ain't much been hungry." David sensed his uneasiness.

"Just things a happenin'." The old man shifted the conversation from himself. "How you been since your lady gone?"

David sighed. "Lost. And so lonely I could bust."

"I am sorry, David. Truly sorry."

"These are strange days. I have been having crazy thoughts lately."

"What kind of thoughts?"

"About my mother. I believe she is still alive."

"Miss Catherine told me 'bout the letter Mary-Anne found at the angel."

"I have considered going to Chicago to find her. There are just so many unanswered questions."

Lawrence nodded understandingly. "We all got things under our skin. Everybody does. Like a glass sliver. Can't see nothin' there, but it works its way in deeper until it gets to festerin' and hurts so that we're ready to just cut the whole thing out."

David poured himself another glass.

"Comes a time that everyone needs to find their answers. Need to connect with their past. You ain't crazy, David, you just filled with the spirit of Elijah."

"What is that?"

"Like the Bible talk 'bout. Turnin' of the children's hearts to the parents'."

David looked down and frowned. "Then I get to thinking that I should let it go—maybe there is nothing to be gained. Maybe my mother was like MaryAnne—she fell out of love."

Lawrence groaned incredulously. "MaryAnne never stopped lovin' you. Lord, David, you talk 'bout love like it a hole. Somethin' you can fall in and out of."

"Isn't it?"

His aged face further wrinkled in indignation. "That ain't love at all, just squirrel fever. Just a storm of emotions." Lawrence grimaced. "Man sees a pretty skirt and calls it love. Most women folk ain't much smarter. Give more credence to butterflies than friendship. Real love's ain't that way. It's more like a tree or plant or somethin'."

"How is that?"

"Grows if you take mind of it. But it takes work and sacrifices. No one stand back of a neglected tree and watch it die and say, 'Guess that tree just ain't suppose to live.' Only a fool would talk like that. But people do it all the time with their loves."

David turned the ideology over in his mind, then abetted its acceptance with another drink. "What of you, Lawrence? How is it that you never loved a woman?"

"Never said I didn't love no woman." His voice suddenly took on a faraway quality. "Loved just one woman my whole life." He lowered his head in sadness. ". . . loved me too."

David stared at his friend in astonishment. "You have never spoken of a woman before."

The name fell reverentially from his lips. "Margaret."

"Margaret," David echoed. "Catherine said that you spoke of her."

Lawrence didn't look up.

"Who was this woman?"

"My greatest love."

"Why weren't you married?"

"Maybe we was."

David could scarcely believe the course of the conversation, and were it not for Lawrence's somber demeanor, he would have believed that Lawrence was fooling with him. Lawrence continued without prompting.

"Margaret was the daughter of a cavalry officer."

David's brow creased. "What is so wrong with an enlisted man marrying an officer's daughter? It must happen all the time."

Lawrence shook his head. "No, it don't happen."

"Why doesn't it?"

Lawrence's voice suddenly flared with annoyance. "Ain't no Negro officers in the U.S. military, David."

David felt foolish for his flawed assumption. "I am sorry, Lawrence."

Lawrence's voice softened. "If I'd of loved her less I'd be with her now. Fine, beautiful woman."

David replied nothing and the conversation withered, supplanted by the lapping of the declining fire in the stove and the chorus of crickets that serenaded the sun's interment. After a few moments, Lawrence broke the silence. His voice was drawn out as if moving along a slower, more weary course. The lantern's orange tongue reflected off the wet streak on Lawrence's cheek.

"There was two women I loved for most my life."

"There is another?"

"There is Sophia," he said, his voice cracking with emotion. He fumbled for his glass, and the conversation again lulled. "I need ask you a favor, David."

"Of course. Anything."

"I don't know how much life this old body of mine has left in it. After I'm gone, if Sophia ever come 'round, I have somethin' for her. Got it put away in the munitions box under my bed."

David glanced over at the cot but could not see the small crate concealed beneath it.

"What is in the box?" David asked.

Lawrence sat quietly for a moment, then said in a trembling voice, "Her answers."

David poured another shot for both men and no more was said of the women.

CHAPTER 10

Christmas

"There is nothing so healing to oneself as to heal another."

DAVID PARKIN'S DIARY.
DECEMBER 26, 1933

On Christmas Eve, the Parkin Machinery Company closed its doors at noon, and, in festive spirits, the employees fled home to their holiday revelry. Only David remained in the quiet building, alone except for the loneliness that darkened his mood as well as his countenance. He returned home in time to see Catherine off, and when her taxi arrived she boarded with great reluctance. Her concern for David was such that she could scarcely bid him farewell.

The winter sun, rendered succinct by the season, had already set when he dressed for the evening's dinner party, and he arrived at Gibbs and Elaine's tardy of the appointed hour. They were joined for dinner by three other couples, making him painfully aware of his own solitude. Gibbs and Elaine tried to cheer him, which made the evening more difficult as there is nothing so certain to exacerbate melancholy as to call attention to it. Three hours after his arrival, he excused himself and made his way home, alone, to the darkened and vacant mansion. Prior to his departure, a rare winter rain had commenced, and the encroaching clouds had blackened out the moon's reflection and wet the landscape. To David, the drenched city had never seemed so dark.

To his wonderment, as he unlocked the front door to his house, he heard the sweet, muted strains of a piano. He gently shut the door behind himself and followed the music down the darkened corridor to the conservatory and peered through the open doorway. Catherine sat at the ebony grand piano, partially visible through its raised hood. Her eyes were closed as she moved to the swells of the music—the repercussions filled the room, bathing it in gentle and healing waves. The room was lit only by a cluster of thick-stemmed candles, their bases encircled by holly leaves. David quietly sat down just inside the doorway while Catherine continued to play, moved only by the music's pull. She gently touched the song's last note and held down the key, relishing the tone as a taste.

"Rachmaninoff was MaryAnne's favorite," David said softly.

At his voice, Catherine let out a small gasp.

"David, how long have you sat there?"

"I didn't mean to startle you," he said. "Just a few moments."

She covered the keys. "I couldn't begin to count the number of times I've played that song for her . . . whenever she was sad." She felt bad for the observation. "What are you doing home?"

"I should ask you the same."

She walked around the piano and sat down next to him. "I didn't want to spend Christmas anywhere else. Or with anyone else." Her countenance lightened. "And don't think that I am pitying you. My motives are entirely selfish."

"Of course they are," David replied in jest.

"Then you would not be averse to joining me in a cup of wassail?"

"Not at all."

She returned with two teacups, handed one to David, then sat back down next to him. The fragrance of cloves filled the air.

"Are you feeling any better?"

"I feel lonely. No offense, Catherine."

"I understand. I feel homesick for MaryAnne, too. Loneliness is always worse at Christmastime." She sipped the hot drink. "Is this your worst Christmas ever?"

David frowned. "No. The year my mother left was the worst. All I asked for that Christmas was to have my mother back. I don't know if I thought St. Nick would bring her back . . ." He smiled sadly. "I truly believed that she would come back." He suddenly looked up, his face showing the pain of the day. "It's still early. Ask me tomorrow."

Catherine moved the conversation to something more cheerful. "What was your best Christmas?"

"My last Christmas with MaryAnne and Andrea. Andrea was at that age that she could sense the spirit of the holiday. Everything was tinsel and magic. Every bauble was for her. I felt it through her. That is the amazing gift of childhood." His words floated reminiscently. "How about you? What was your best Christmas?"

Catherine smiled thoughtfully. "The Christmas when I was nine. My family never had much. That Christmas I got a rag doll my mother had made from scraps she had saved from her sewing. My oldest brother had brought home a pine, and we made our own decorations—painted walnut shells and paper snowflakes. I was so excited you would have thought that I had spent Christmas at the Van- derbilts'. Later on that day, my uncle, who lived just down the road from us, came to the house. He told my mother about a family whose father had been killed only two weeks earlier, leaving them destitute. My mother asked us children if we would be willing to share our Christmas. We all knew what that meant as we only had one present." She smiled. "There was a little, flaxen-haired girl about my age. I'll never forget the look in her eyes as I gave her my doll."

David's eyes moistened as he considered the child's sacrifice. "That is truly remarkable, Cather- ine. What was your worst Christmas?"

A wry grin stole across her face. "Same one."

David laughed heartily until his laughter died in a pleased sigh. "Are you going to mass?"

"I think we're too late," Catherine replied. "St. Marks is usually filled by ten."

David glanced at his watch. "I didn't realize the hour was so late."

Catherine just smiled lovingly. She held up her teacup. "To Christmas, David."

David lifted his. "To Christmases past. At least some of them."

Catherine's smile fell as David's toast evoked a pang of sadness.

"Thank you for coming back."

"You're welcome." She kissed him on the cheek, then stood. "I better finish my rum sauce." She stopped at the door's threshold. "You were wrong when you said I hadn't spent Christmas with my family for too long. You and Mary are my family. And I hope she comes back soon."

"Me, too, Catherine."

"Good night, David."

✦

Christmas morning arrived in cheerful declaration by the bells of the Cathedral of the Madeleine and the pleasing fragrance of Christmas sweet breads still hot from the oven—stollen and "Julekake"— filled the downstairs of the Parkin house and could not help but sweeten the home's disposition. The night's rain had turned to snow, and the city was covered in flawless white sheets as smooth as the blue skies above. Catherine smiled as David entered the room.

"Merry Christmas."

"Merry Christmas," he replied jovially.

The kitchen's counters were lined with fluted pies, mincemeat and gooseberry, that awaited the roast goose for their turns in the oven. Two tins of Parker House rolls rose under dishcloths, and a small pan of rum sauce boiled on the stove for the plum pudding which Catherine was preparing to steam.

"So what congregation are you feeding today?"

"Just you, Lawrence, and me."

David sat down at the table. "It is almost a shame to go to so much work for so few people."

"Not when they are people I care about."

David smiled gratefully. "Can I help you with something?"

"You can pick up Lawrence."

"I had already planned on it. I thought I would bring him here early and listen to some records or read to him."

"Well, be sure to eat something. Dinner won't be ready until two."

David snatched a pepparkaker from the counter, placed the cookie in his palm, and struck it with his knuckle. It broke in a half dozen pieces.

"You're hitting it too hard," Catherine said. "Here." She placed a cookie in her palm, made a silent wish, then struck it. It broke in three pieces. She handed the largest of the pieces to David. "You always give the largest piece to someone you love. Then your wish will come true."

"What did you wish for?"

"I think you could guess." She handed a small stack of the cookies to David. "Here. Take these for Lawrence and you to snack on."

David was gone much longer than Catherine had anticipated, and, for a moment, she worried that perhaps something was wrong with Lawrence. When David finally returned it was with great commotion. He walked into the kitchen.

"Catherine, we have some unexpected guests."

Just then a mop-haired boy in tattered dungarees stuck his head into the room. He was followed by a thin, balding man who pulled the boy back by his denim straps. The stranger looked up at Catherine.

"Good Christmas, ma'am."

"Catherine, this is Frank Cobb. The Cobbs are passing through the city and had nowhere to spend Christmas."

"Sorry to impose, Mrs. Parkin. We got stranded in town yesterday. I asked Mr. Parkin if he might have a little work—somethin' to help feed the kids. He offered us to come and spend Christmas dinner with you. We're all mighty grateful."

Catherine smiled. "You are welcome here, Mr. Cobb. And I am Catherine, Mr. Parkin's housekeeper. Mrs. Parkin is out of the country."

"I apologize, ma'am."

"Not at all. How many are there of you?"

"Eight of us. With the baby."

A plain-faced woman came around and stood behind her man. She had desolate eyes that confessed the family's hardship and the burden she bore. She was dressed in a worn gingham dress slipped down over her shoulder as she nursed an infant at her breast. Catherine could not help but feel compassion for the woman.

"This is my wife, Bette."

The woman stooped. "Ma'am."

"Welcome, Bette. It is a pleasure having your family join us. In fact, Mr. Parkin was saying only this morning what a shame it was that we didn't have someone to share this meal with."

"Thank you, ma'am." She glanced around the cluttered kitchen. "Is there somethin' I can do to help in the kitchen? Been a while since I really got to preparin' somethin' more than fry dough or baked beans."

"I could use a good hand. I haven't mashed the turnips yet and the rolls still need basting."

The woman smiled at the invitation to help. ". . . be kind of nice to be in a real kitchen again."

Five children stood quietly out in the large foyer, captivated by the wealth that surrounded them, and the older of the clan kept close eye on the younger, slapping them if they dared touch anything or looked like they were thinking about it. David went out to them carrying a tin canister of pepparkaker. He handed the container to the second oldest. "Would you children like to listen to the radio while you eat these cookies? I think it's about time for *Death Valley Days.*"

The children's faces lit with delight, and the chamber echoed a chorus of "thanks, mister" and "much obliged." While the children happily congregated at the foot of the instrument, cookies in both hands, the men—David, Lawrence, Frank, and his oldest son, Leroy—resigned themselves to the parlor. The young man surveyed the room with wide eyes.

"Gee, mister. You got more than one radio set?" he asked with astonishment. "Ain't that the Ritz. Just listen anywhere you please. I'm gonna have me a place like this one day."

Frank Cobb scowled. "You hush up or you can go sit with the children. Ain't you learned a single manner."

The boy flushed. "Sorry, mister."

David smiled. "It's okay, Leroy."

Frank leaned forward. "Now this here Negro. He your help man?"

Lawrence chuckled. "If I am, he shorely could do much better."

"Lawrence is my friend," David said. He leaned forward and opened a decanter of whiskey. "Care for something to drink?"

"Well, don't mind if I do."

David poured a drink for all four of them, and Leroy looked especially proud to be drinking with the men.

"So what brings you through Salt Lake City?"

"Truth is, we headed to California, but we run out of fare for the train and couldn't buy tickets for all of us. So we thought we'd find a place for the missus and the kids, and Leroy and I'd go on and send back for them. Hear there's always something need'n to be picked in California. Hate to split up the family, but you gotta do what you gotta."

David frowned. He knew the way of the plantations and the greed that ran them.

"Have you had any luck finding anything here for your wife?"

"We've only been in town a day, but we thinkin' somethin'll turn up. Just gotta."

David looked suddenly thoughtful. "You know, splitting up a family is a hard thing. It would be better if you stayed together."

"If you ain't got three dollars for a ticket then you ain't got three dollars."

"Perhaps there is something I could do."

A look of distress flashed across Frank's hard, sunbaked face. "Don't mean to be ungrateful, Mr. Parkin, but no Cobb has ever taken charity, and I don't mean to be the first. We're hard workers and respectable folk. Always have been. If we hadn't lost our land to the bankers we'd still be plowin' it."

"I'm not offering charity, Frank. I'm offering a business proposition. That's the way things work in the world of high finance."

The man stared at him without comprehension.

"It's like betting on hog bellies or corn futures. I'm betting that you're going to do well in Califor-

nia. All I'm saying is that any business needs a little seed money. So I'll give you enough to get your
family there and a little to settle with. Say, two hundred dollars."

The man looked astonished.

"Then, when things are comfortable I expect you
to pay me back. With interest."

"How you know I wouldn't just run off with your
money?"

"I can tell what kind of man you are, Frank. I've
made my living reading people."

"Well, what if things don't work out? I mean
they're a gonna, but what if . . ."

"That's business, Frank. No one has ever given
me a guarantee. Certainly is no more risky than the
stock market."

"Well, I can't argue that."

Leroy watched his father with great interest.
"You gonna do it, ain't you, Pap?"

"Well, I'll give it a thought."

"You give it a thought," David said. "My invest-
ment portfolio could use a little diversification."

"Don't know what that means, but I'll give it a
thought. You got a contract? I know them bankers
in the finance world got contracts."

"What's paper if people aren't honorable? I do
business with a handshake."

Frank leaned back, and Leroy looked at him anxiously. "I like the way you do business, Mister
Parkin. I think we can make a deal. How much interest you thinkin'?"

"I don't know. I'm not giving any handouts, now. I want at least two percent."

Lawrence said, "David's no fool. He's gonna get two percent somewhere."

Frank thought some more. "Okay. Two percent. As soon as we got a roof over our head."

David hid his smile behind his glass. "Couldn't ask for more than that."

Bette Cobb came into the foyer and called the family to supper. When they had all gathered around the table Catherine said, "Would you mind if I blessed the food, David?"

"Not at all."

They all bowed their heads.

"Father, for this bounty we thank you. And for this day and the gift of your Son. Bless MaryAnne while she is away. Bless the Cobb family with health and safety and in all their travels. In the name of our Lord. Amen."

The room resounded with "Amens."

"Much obliged," Frank said.

The family loaded their plates as the platters moved around the large table—creamed turnips, carrots with glaze, lutefisk and limpa bread, and hot Parker House rolls. The children's eyes were wide as they anxiously awaited permission to start in.

"Go on," Catherine said. "We've said grace. No reason to hold back."

"Shore's some fancy food," Frank said, raising a fork.

"Catherine's family is from Scandinavia," Bette explained. "Brought lots of traditions with them."

"Best meal of the year," Lawrence said. "Start lookin' forward to it the day the first snow flies."

Catherine blushed. "Bette helped me," she said.

The family ate ravenously, and David and Catherine watched them happily. When they had been through several helpings, Catherine and Bette brought out the pies to the mutual acclaim of the diners, and they were cut and placed on small plates and, along with the sweet breads, were handed around the table. As they ate, David leaned over and whispered something to Catherine. She smiled as David excused himself from the table and disappeared from the room. When he returned he had a large box in his hands.

"St. Nick must have known you would all be here because he left these toys, and I don't have anyone to play with them. Let's see. We have a pretty doll here. Just right for . . . Amanda. And another for Sharon."

The two girls squealed. Catherine's eyes moistened as she watched David hand out Andrea's toys.

"Here's a stuffed bear." David looked into the child's eager face. "I believe this is for Phillip. Let's see. There is one present left. A monkey. Anyone here need a monkey?"

"Is it for me?" Thomas asked.

"I'm certain it must be." He handed the gift to the boy.

"Thank you, mister," he said as he clutched the animal tightly.

As the women cleared off the table, the children ran off to play with their new treasures, and David led Lawrence to the parlor to nap in front of the fireplace on the large sofa. David then went to his den and chair and turned on the radio. There was a soft knock at his door.

"Mister Parkin?"

David looked up. Leroy stood in the doorway. A grave look of anxiety blanketed his face.

"Hello, Leroy."

"Need to talk with you," he said tensely.

David motioned to a chair. "Of course. Sit down."

Leroy walked to the chair but stood behind it, nervously swaying from foot to foot.

"'Bout what you said earlier. 'Bout the two percent and all. We may be Okies, but I been around some. That's just hooey."

David leaned back in his seat, carefully studying the boy's expression.

"I want to know why you'd go givin' us two hunderd dollars we both know you ain't never gonna see again."

"Why do you think?"

"Don't know what to think. My pap's just a farmer. He don't know 'bout finance and stuff. He still don't know how it was them bankers came and took our land. I gotta tell him like it is, Mister Parkin. Gotta tell him somethin' ain't right."

"I don't think you should do that, Leroy."

Leroy answered defensively, "Why shouldn't I?"

"People like your father are the mortar that holds this world together. And it's their dignity that holds them together. Say you go on and tell him that it's really just charity I'm offering. Then, if he takes the money he loses himself. Or, if he decides to decline the money, he loses his family. Either way a good man loses. You take his dignity from him and you're as damned a fool as the bankers."

Leroy could not reply.

"Your father's not *just* a farmer. He's not *just* anything. A man's worth isn't measured by a bank register or a diploma, Leroy. It's about integrity. You remember that."

The boy looked embarrassed. "I'm sorry, Mister Parkin."

"It's all right, Leroy. You just care about your folks. There's not a thing wrong with that."

Leroy nodded thoughtfully as he quietly walked out of the room.

✦

As night fell David found Catherine on the landing.

"I have been looking for you. Why is your dress wet?"

"Bette and I bathed the children, then washed their clothes. She had never seen an electric washing machine."

"You look exhausted."

"I don't think I have ever worked so hard on a Christmas."

"I'm sorry. I'll make it up to you."

"No you won't. I wouldn't trade today for anything. That was kind of you to invite the Cobbs to spend the night."

"Are they all down?"

"The children are asleep. Leroy is still in the parlor listening to the radio. Frank and Bette are in the east guest room."

"Frank wants to leave at sunup."

"I'll make sure they have a good breakfast. And I'll pack something for the train. Bette told me about the 'business deal.' That was really good of you, David. You have made a difference."

"It's only one family. There are millions of Cobbs out there. It is silly to think it made a difference."

"It made a difference to them."

David nodded slowly.

"Where is Lawrence?" Catherine asked.

"I took him home."

"I thought he was going to spend the night."

"He wouldn't. He just complained that he gets lost in a big house like this and knocks everything over. He's really afraid that we're conspiring to move him out of his shanty."

"MaryAnne would have been so pleased with today," Catherine said. She suddenly sighed. "I'm sorry. I shouldn't have spoken of her."

"You don't need to be afraid to speak of MaryAnne. Besides, today was your doing, really."

"How so?"

"The story you told me last night—about the rag doll. You reminded me that sometimes the best remedy for a broken heart is to use it."

"I don't think you ever forgot."

David looked down. "Yes, I did."

"You said you were looking for me."

"I want to give you your Christmas present." He reached into his pocket and brought out a small crushed-velvet box. The sight of the box made Catherine's heart skip. She felt uncomfortable taking it from him.

"Open it."

She carefully lifted its lid. Inside was a petite, brilliant, sapphire and diamond brooch. She gasped. "David."

"Merry Christmas."

A tear rolled down her cheek, and for several minutes she was unable to speak. "I have never owned a diamond."

"No woman, especially you, Catherine, should go through life without a diamond."

She could not take her eyes from it. "What will I wear it with? Oh, David. Is it really for me?"

"Thank you for Christmas, Catherine." He kissed her on the cheek, then went off to his room.

CHAPTER 11

The Tommy Knockers

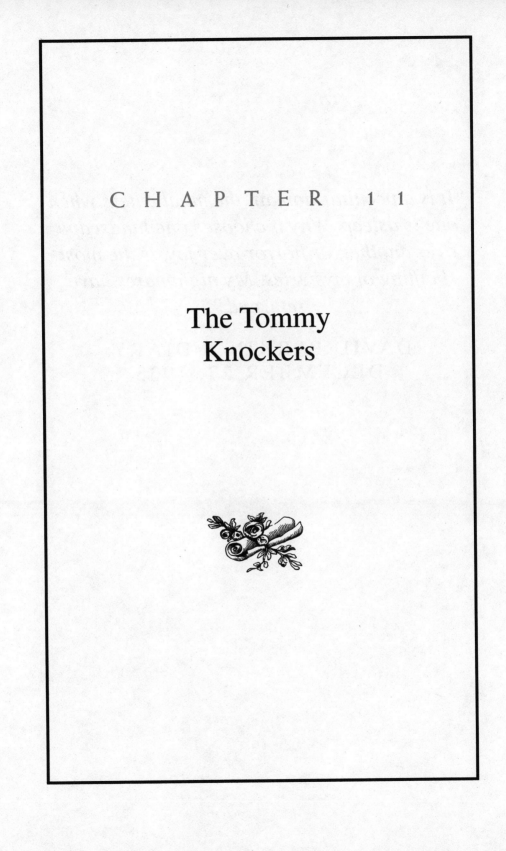

"It is a peculiar domain the mind enters when one is asleep. Why it chooses one landscape over another, or horror over joy, is the most baffling of mysteries. My nightmares have returned."

DAVID PARKIN'S DIARY.
DECEMBER 27, 1933

It was not the first time that the same nightmare had plagued David's sleep. The nightmare was staged two hundred feet below the earth's surface and always with the same performers: a small boy, his face soiled from the mine's clay walls, and an elderly Cornishman, his oily face gleaming from the amber radiance of the kerosene lanterns that hung from the shaft's shoring timbers. The small boy stared anxiously into the foreigner's squint eyes as the flickering lanterns danced their shadows against the earthen walls in demonic contortions. The musty odor of dirt filled the nostrils, and the only sound was the distant crying of men and the slight, incessant tapping echo that rose from somewhere below. From the black.

The boy's expression asked the question without voice.

"It's the Tommy knockers, lad. Poundin' their pickaxes."

"What's a Tommy knocker?"

". . . souls of miners swallowed in the shafts."

The boy looked fearfully at the man. "What does it mean?"

The old man's lips pursed in a cruel smile. "Why, it means there's gonna be a cave-in." The jaundiced face suddenly erupted in laughter. "Run, lad! . . . Run!"

The boy bolted, frantically pumping his twig legs between the vacant steel tracks of the ore cars. Behind him, from the depths of the mine, a low rumble emerged, rising in growing intensity like an approaching avalanche. The hysterical laughter of the Englishman was drowned out by the mounting roar, and the subterranean walls trembled beneath its groan.

Ahead, the child could see the distant light of the mine's mouth, partially eclipsed by a form that stood at the entrance. It was his mother's form, her arms outstretched to catch her son. "Run, David! Run!"

Suddenly, thirty yards ahead, a thick, wooden rafter collapsed, and a wall of rock and dirt cascaded before him, followed by a river of muddy sludge that surfed over the splintered timber's back, flooding downward into the pit.

"Mama!"

All light vanished and David fell in the torrential mud, grasping for a handhold in the craggy walls, lest the current sweep him into the earth's bowels.

"Mama!" he screamed again. But there was no answer. And even the suffocating walls of the cavern returned no echo.

✦

David jolted up in bed. His heart raced as he gasped for breath. At the sound of his cry, Catherine had come to his room, her distress manifest across her face. "David . . ."

He looked towards her, and Catherine felt a pang of apprehension. His eyes were wild and his chest continued to heave. She walked to the side of his bed. "Are you all right?"

He exhaled. "It was just another bad dream."

". . . you were calling for your mother."

David stared at her as if the revelation was beyond his comprehension, then, recounting the vision, groaned as he rolled back into his pillow.

"When did the nightmares return?"

David hesitantly replied. "When you gave me the letter."

Catherine sat down at the foot of his bed with one leg crossed beneath her. In the eight years she had lived in the mansion before David had married, Catherine had come to expect the nightmares and the regularity of David's scream echoing throughout the house's dark hallways. She had come to dread the night terrors almost as much as did David. Almost miraculously, the nightmares had ceased with MaryAnne's arrival, and, after twenty years, Catherine had forgotten about the once nightly phenomenon. She did not welcome its return. She rested her head in her hand.

"Then MaryAnne was right. I should not have shared the letter."

David gently took her hand. "No, you did right. No matter how painful, the truth is rarely a disservice."

Neither spoke, and the room's only sound was the clock. Suddenly Catherine looked up.

"Do you remember when I told you about the hobos that come to the house almost every day to ask for food?"

David looked at her quizzically, unable to guess what the anecdote had to do with the moment.

"Yes."

"The Monday last, another one came by. I made him a jam sandwich, and he asked if he could eat it out on the porch. A few minutes later my curiosity got the better of me, and I went back out and asked him why it was that he, like the others, walked past three other homes and came directly to our place to ask for food." A vague smile surfaced on Catherine's lips. "He pointed to the large sycamore at the corner of Fifth Avenue and said, 'See that tree yonder? There's a sign that someone nailed to it says the fourth house on this street will feed you.'"

"A sign?"

"One of those hobos must have put it up for those that came after," Catherine said. Her modest smile receded. "My point is, there is always a reason that things happen. When MaryAnne showed me your mother's letter she said its arrival at this time was rather peculiar. I didn't know what she meant at the time. But I think that I do now. I think there is a reason that the letter came when it did."

"And what might that be?"

"Maybe that it's time that you come to peace with her."

David considered her theory.

"I stopped by the cemetery to see the sexton as you requested. About a month back, as he was closing the yard, he came across an old woman crying at Andrea's angel. She left a letter and a flower."

An astonished look crept over his face. "Then it was my mother."

"Perhaps. As I grow older I find that I become more fatalistic. Looking back over my life, I believe that it has been guided by unseen forces. And that I have been showered with clues to direct my path."

"What kind of forces?"

"I'm not certain. God. His angels. Maybe just some great universal force of truth. Whatever you call it, there is something that shapes and directs our lives. I am certain of it. We can ignore the clues, we all do from time to time, sometimes we don't even see them. But I don't think that we, or our lives, will be complete without them."

David spoke seriously. "That is exactly how I have felt. Incomplete. Like an unfinished puzzle with a piece of me out there waiting to be found." A look of pain crossed his face. "And yet, with all my heart, I fear it."

"You fear that you won't find your answer?"

"No, I fear its discovery. To come face to face with my mother and learn who I really am."

"David, what your mother is, or was, has nothing to do with who you are."

David shook his head. "It has everything to do with who I am. Especially now. My mother's leaving is the reason I cannot forgive myself for losing my own daughter." He hung his head. "And it is why I fear to go after MaryAnne."

Catherine squeezed David's hand. "Then you must search out your mother. If for no other reason than to exorcise your demons."

"How could I hope to find her?"

Catherine spoke with uncharacteristic assuredness. "If it is to be, you will find her."

David looked up at the dim ceiling as the night's weariness enveloped the room. Catherine's countenance glowed with empathy as she gazed into his darkened face. When David spoke again it was with resolution.

"After the new year I will go to Chicago."

CHAPTER 12

Rose

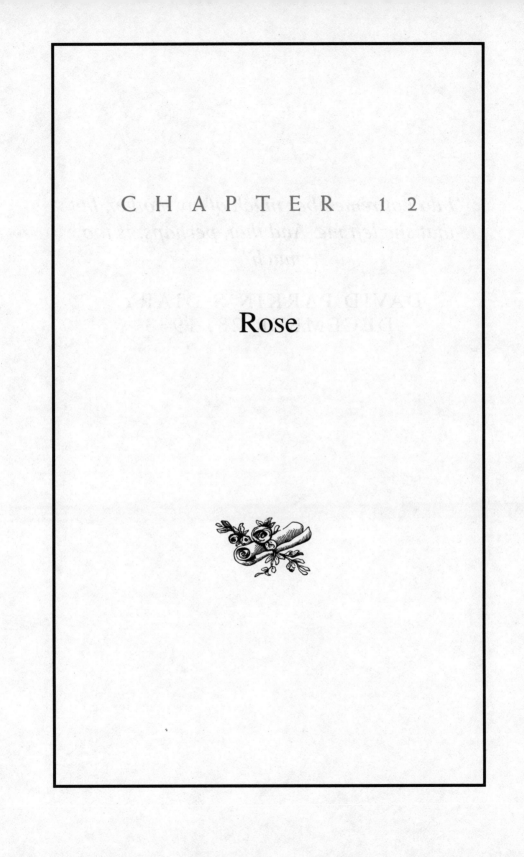

"I do not remember much of my mother, but that she left me. And that, perhaps, is too much."

DAVID PARKIN'S DIARY.
DECEMBER 28, 1933

FORTY-EIGHT YEARS PREVIOUS. 1885, GRASS VALLEY, CALIFORNIA

Rosalyn Parkin folded in the leg-of-mutton sleeves of a threadbare satin dress, creased the garment in thirds, then pressed it tightly against the print interior of the Saratoga trunk. She need not be so efficient. She had come to northern California a decade earlier with three cases of wardrobe—the costumes of her trade—velvet and satin dance hall dresses, tight-waisted and full-bodiced with the risqué necklines of the burlesque, teased by boas of swansdown and fur: lynx and chinchilla. In the last decade, the garments had frayed and faded, were used as rags, or converted into a child's clothing. What remained of the wardrobe now fit too comfortably in the lone trunk.

She surveyed the room a final time for anything she could not part with from the last decade. The pre-dawn darkness concealed nothing. There was nothing to hide.

The room consisted of a few pieces of scavenged furniture, a chest of drawers, and a steel-banded cedar chest, both jettisoned with unfulfilled dreams by miners who had abandoned the small town, cured of their gold lust by austerity's stark tutorial.

The abode's slat walls were bare except for two faded playbills set in place and adored quietly with the reverence afforded religious icons: a color lithograph of the Kiralfy Brothers' performance of *Black Crook,* of which she had attended, and a parchment letterpress of *Macbeth,* where she had represented the role of Fleance.

She closed and buckled the trunk, then lifted it from the bed's stuffed, meadow grass mattress. There was not a thing she could not leave behind.

As she emerged from the dim room into the corridor, a cry, thin-voiced and undulating, emanated from the shadows. It froze her.

"Mama."

Through the pre-dawn blackness, Rose could make out the outline of her six-year-old son curled up in the corner of the hallway. The boy was feminine in form, petite and dark, his skin tanned from a life spent beneath the torrid California sun.

The child was created in her image. His eyes, like hers, were almond-shaped and azure blue, resting upon high, sculptured cheeks. His coffee-colored hair, matching hers to the tint, fell long to his shoulders, and, to the boy's shame, curled at the ends in sienna ringlets.

"I thought you were at the mine with your father, David."

The boy stared malevolently at the trunk, as if it were taking his mother away, instead of the inverse.

"Where are you going, Mama?"

She set the trunk down and approached her child, crouching before him.

"To Nevada City," she answered in partial truth. She would hire a hack the four miles to the Nevada City depot, board the Central Pacific to Colfax, where the tracks would change direction, conveying her through a myriad of mining towns before assaulting the great hewn stone terraces of the Sierra Nevadas—the last great obstacle to her escape from California.

The boy's forehead wrinkled. In the instinctual premonitions of survival—as animals flee before natural calamities—children, too, perceive when their world is threatened. He pushed at a tear which crept down his cheek. "When will you come home?"

Rose gazed at the boy solemnly.

"I don't know," she finally said, and it was quiet except for the babbling of the creek that fell behind their shanty home.

The boy sniffed, then rubbed his nose on the arm of the tattered cotton shirt he wore, then, inexplicably, relinquished his fear, as if in acceptance of an unknown fate.

"Will you bring me a molasses stick?"

"I will bring you two."

A hopeful smile stretched across the boy's face. "You won't be gone so long, will you?"

She brushed back the hair from the boy's forehead, but did not answer. David lifted the small toy he held. A music box carousel, carved in wood and hand-painted in oil pigments that had begun their desertion of the wood. The boy's treasure.

"Take my horses, Mama. To keep company."

The magnanimity of the gesture was not lost on her. She hesitated, then received the toy from his outstretched hand, avoiding the ardent gaze of his pleading eyes.

"Be sure to bring it back, Mama. Don't lose it."

She took a deep breath, then rose to her feet. Taking up her bag, she walked out of the home. Suddenly, David became frightened and cried out after her, "Mama."

But she did not return, and the child never considered that he might not see her again.

CHAPTER 13

A Chance
Encounter

"Chicago boasts a profusion of theaters and cabarets—myriads more than I had presumed. One often does not realize the bulk of the haystack or the meagerness of the needle until one has sorted the first bale."

DAVID PARKIN'S DIARY.
JANUARY 6, 1934

The five-hundred-and-thirty-ton San Francisco Zephyr crawled beneath a flat, grey ceiling of stratus clouds into the Chicago Union depot thirty-seven hours from its Salt Lake City departure, heralding its arrival with the fanfare of its hydraulic brakes.

The bedouin cast of porters heaved trunks and cases to the wood-planked platform where bags were claimed, hands extended, and tips bestowed, pocketed by the performers who disappeared back onto their moving stage for the next act. David, lugging his only case, emerged from the train into the brace of the cold Chicago air.

A forest of paper has been inked on the Chicago of the early century when America's second city was its first—as much an ideology as a locale—a symbol of a country's tenacity. Even the city's name was canonized in the vernacular of the era. If someone or -thing looked hard or tough it was deemed "Chicago."

David had not been to the sprawling metropolis for nearly a decade and was astonished by its burgeoning growth, in population as well as architecture. Wide grilled automobiles filled the tar roads or parked at their curbs, where they served as bleachers for the unemployed and vagabond who watched the city's motion with quiet, hungry eyes. Others, more resigned to their situation, gathered in small quorums to play hands of tattered cards or patient, endless games of bottle-cap checkers on chalked concrete sidewalks.

It was a city of paradox, from the sidewalks, where apples were sold by the hungry to the well fed, to the rising skyscrapers that optimistically stretched heavenward, casting their shadows on the homeless below.

Out of the depot crowd broke a small boy, mop-haired, angular in form, preceded by the wood-crate cart he pushed. His speed was fueled by the competition of dozens of other men and boys who raced to the trains like a flashing tide of piranha.

"Carry your bag, mister?"

David judged the child ten or eleven, nearly out-weighed by the bag he proposed to carry.

"Can you lift it?"

"Yes, sir," the boy replied, raising his small frame—his protruded chest made absurd by the depression it left of his stomach.

"Just to the curb, then."

"Swell."

When he had traveled the distance to the street, the boy, left breathless by his journey, held out his hand. David produced a silver dollar. "For your trouble."

For a moment the boy stared at the sterling orb in

disbelief, then, with the wariness of a sparrow pecking a morsel of bread from an open palm, he snatched the coin.

"Thank you, sir!" he shouted, fleeing with his fortune.

David smiled as he watched the boy disappear into the amorphous crowd, then turned back to the street and lifted his hand to a yellow cab for a ride to the Drake Hotel.

✦

Of the city's grand hotels, the world's for that matter, few shone with the refulgence of the Drake on Chicago's gold coast, a limestone edifice rising thirteen floors above the lapping waves of Lake Michigan. Since the munificent fanfare of its opening in 1920, the hotel had been the favorite of the city's visiting dignitaries—the kings and presidents, queens and first ladies—as well as the celebrities of the era. The hotel's plush ballrooms served as forums for the country's great bands, broadcast to the rest of the world from WGN radio, located on the upper level of the H-shaped building.

David's cab sided up to the hotel's front curb, shadowed beneath an iron canopy which hung from chains over the hotel's attendant bronze sentinels—lanterns of winged dragons, borrowed from the crest of the brothers Drake. A top-hatted doorman in a black uniform with bright crimson leg-striping attended to the curbside door, slightly bowing. "Welcome to the Drake, sir."

David paid the driver, then stepped from the car to the pavement. While the driver surrendered David's trunk to the awaiting bell captain, David climbed the steps into the luxuriant, crowded lobby of the hotel, amidst the aristocratic swoon of the perfumed gentry, attired in the costumes and furs of their status. The Depression did not exist inside the Drake, in decor or humanity, and as the world groaned beneath the weight of financial distress, the Drake's gilded walls rendered its suffering imperceptible.

The interior walls of the lobbyway were marble or wood-paneled in rich oak with burled parquet insets, set between intricate alabaster moldings. The floor was a collage of swirling Tennessee marble, accented by ebony inlays, overlaid, in the winter, by thick, vermilion carpets. Two crystal chandeliers, each a man's length in breadth, hung from high ceilings above twin, round-topped tables, each sustaining a sterling flute with a large spray of dried florals. The chandeliers hung thirteen feet above the floor—eye-level to the lobby's terraced sitting room, where guests would take tea and look down upon the high-hatted registrants in hopes of a celebrity sighting.

A clerk, tall, capped with a shock of brilliant red hair, greeted him. "At your service, sir."

"The name is David Parkin. I have a reservation."

"Welcome to the Drake, Mr. Parkin." The clerk stepped back from the counter as he shuffled through a register, then retrieved a set of brass keys stowed in the pigeonholed wall behind him. "You are reserved a suite, Mr. Parkin. Your accommodations are prepared. I took the liberty of having a fruit basket delivered to your room."

"Thank you."

"You will be staying in suite seven twenty-nine." The clerk handed David the key. "You have an extraordinary view of the lake. The elevator is just south of the lobby."

At the clerk's summons a bellboy approached.

"May I assist with your bag, sir?"

The clerk answered for him. "Please see Mr. Parkin to suite seven twenty-nine."

"Right away, sir."

David handed the man a quarter with the instruction to just leave the bag inside his room, then sauntered over to the concierge's counter. The concierge set down his telephone.

"Good evening, sir. How may I serve you?"

"I need a list of the city's theaters."

"That would be quite a listing, sir. Perhaps there is a specific production you are interested in."

"I am trying to find someone. I may have to visit every theater in the area."

"I see," he replied with a smile. "You have your work cut out for you. The most complete listing would be the telephone directory. I believe that I have an extra copy." He crouched below the counter, then rose, clutching a thick book in his hands, thumbed through the pages until he found the designation of theaters. "Here you are, sir."

David examined the directory. The theater listing was nearly three pages in length.

"As I stated, it is quite extensive. However, many of the theaters are now used exclusively for moving picture shows."

"It appears as though I'll be a guest of your hotel longer than I had anticipated." David tucked the directory under his arm. "Thank you for your help."

"My pleasure, sir."

"Is there a nearby restaurant you would recommend?"

"The Charlie Whiting band is performing in the Gold Coast dining room."

"Perhaps something more intimate."

"I would recommend the French Room. Just past the palm court and to the right of the mezzanine."

"Thank you."

David made his way through the crowded corridors to the restaurant. The French Room was smaller than most of the Drake's other dining rooms, dimly lit and partitioned by large columns accented with white moldings and flourishes. Windows, divided in small, abundant panes, revealed the lakeshore beach rendered vacant by the season. French doors opened to an outer terrace where dancing was held in the warmer months. It was sparsely occupied for a weekend evening.

David ordered his meal, then laid out a map of

the city and on the back of a cloth napkin began the work of dividing the theaters by city regions. When his meal arrived, he closed the directory. He ate slowly as he looked out over the dying day—the dusk obscuring the lake's dark waters, visible only in the outline of the bleached swells. He wondered about MaryAnne; where she was and if she thought of him as frequently as he thought of her. And if her heart hurt too. He finished his meal, ordered black coffee and cherries jubilee, and only departed the dining room after a boisterous crowd entered the tranquil restaurant, occupying two nearby tables.

The hallway outside the French Room reverberated from the blare of the Gold Coast Room's brass band. The ballroom was the Drake's, as well as the city's, premier dance floor, and the biggest bands in America aspired to its venue. The spacious ballroom, currently dressed in gold and cream, changed its name twice yearly as it was repainted for the season. In the warmer months it was the Silver Forest Room as its winter hues yielded to cooler tones of silver and blue.

The ballroom's double doors were open to allow circulation of both air and guests, and the hallway outside was crowded with flushed dancers and the more sedate, who came to see and hear the famous bands without investing their own activity. As David pressed his way through the crowd, a woman brushed past him, then spun around.

"David!"

"Dierdre?"

She shouted over the din, "What in the world are you doing here?"

"I am a guest at the hotel. What are you doing here?"

"All the great bands come to the Drake. I come here every Friday."

Suddenly, a man, tall and well-built, with flaxen hair curled in carefully manicured swells, stepped forward and took Dierdre's arm, asserting his claim on the woman. He was immaculately dressed in a striped suit with cuffed, baggy trousers and a jacket with sharp, thin lapels.

"Robert, this is my friend David. He is from Salt Lake City."

"A real pleasure," the man lied, obviously more annoyed than pleased. "I only went to get you a drink. I didn't expect you would be absent upon my return."

Dierdre smiled. "Relax, Robert, I just went for some air. It was getting too hot in there." She straightened his lapel, and her drawl thickened. "Come on, let's go back inside." She glanced back at David. "How long are you in town, David?"

"Maybe a week. Possibly longer."

"We must get together. I will ring you."

The man glared at David before offering his arm to Dierdre.

David waved her off. "Go dance."

Dierdre smiled. "Toodleoo," she replied, then let her rankled date lead her back to the ballroom.

✦

"Within a few hours of my arrival in Chicago I chanced to meet Dierdre. I can only wonder how this fits into Catherine's theory."

DAVID PARKIN'S DIARY. JANUARY 6, 1934

✦

Early the next morning, David began the first of his calls to the theaters. His first dozen attempts taught him that those who answered the phones at theaters and those nearer the stage were of two different breeds. Those who greeted him often knew little more than the price of a ticket and their stage's current inhabitants, and sometimes not even that. Around noon, he went out and visited several theaters closest to the Drake. The only useful bit of information he garnered was discouraging. He learned that there was such turnover in the business that a performance just a decade earlier might as well been of a different century.

When he returned to the hotel at around six, he found a message waiting for him. Dierdre had invited him to dinner, assumed the engagement for seven that very evening, and requested no confirmation. He went up to his room and changed his shirt.

At a quarter of the hour, Dierdre arrived in the hotel's lobby dressed with her usual panache. She wore a form-fitting, black velvet dress with an ivory, lace collar, and an Empress Eugénie was strategically dipped over her left brow. She clutched a red-sequined handbag with both hands. When she did not find David, she patiently sat down at the end of a tucked, red velvet love seat, seemingly content in her examination of the passing guests—most of whom were very content to examine her back. When David arrived five minutes later, she hailed him from across the room.

"David!" she called. She rose as David approached. "It is so nice seeing you again," she said jubilantly. "It was such a surprise bumping into you last evening."

"I was surprised that you recognized me. It was only one dance."

"One and a half." She smiled. "And you are not as forgettable as you think."

David smiled bashfully. "I feel a little embarrassed."

"Whatever for?"

"I wasn't sure if . . ." He paused, feeling suddenly awkward. "Well, perhaps you had expected me to call."

"I had hoped," she replied candidly. "I am just glad you would meet me for dinner. So where would you like to go?"

"It's your city."

"Do you care for German cuisine? There is a superb restaurant and brewery just a few miles from here, on Adams."

"Do they serve sauerbraten?"

"With spaetzle and sauerkraut."

"Perfect."

"Swell." She took his arm. "Bennie is parked out front."

"Bennie?"

"My chauffeur."

At the front curb of the hotel idled a hunter green, chrome-grilled Duesenberg sedan, a full fourteen feet in length. The Duesenberg was the rare and luxurious automobile of czars and presidents and, as such, procured its own celebrity status which it lavished upon all who occupied its coach. David had admired the vehicle, as did all who knew automobiles, but had never before set foot in one. At their approach, a uniformed chauffeur, a black man of medium build, scrambled to their door. David followed Dierdre inside.

The automobile's coachwork was of the finest leather with adornments of polished hardwood and ivory inset with sterling silver. The rear side of the driver's seat had instrumented panels duplicating the driver's dashboard.

"A Duesenberg?"

"It's Daddy's car. You expected a DeSoto?"

"No. It's perfectly you."

Dierdre smiled wryly. "I will take that as a compliment."

The chauffeur closed the door behind them.

✦

The Berghoff was a Chicago landmark and boasted a heritage as rich as the ale it brewed. The restaurant's interior was attired in the dress and spirit of the Oktoberfest, and trophies of boars heads and wide-antlered hart hung from the walls of ocher wood. When they had settled in, ordered, and discussed the glory and pitfalls of the cuisine, Dierdre turned the conversation more intimate.

"How was your Christmas?"

"Mostly lonely."

"I'm sorry to hear that. You should have come to Chicago. During the holidays there are just hordes of people downtown. I don't know where they all come from."

"Sometimes there is nothing so lonely as a crowd."

Dierdre understood and smiled.

"Fortunately, I did have Catherine."

"Is Catherine your sister?"

"Catherine is my housekeeper."

Dierdre lit a cigarette and took a drag. "So what business brings you to Chicago?"

"Not business. I came for personal reasons."

She turned her head to expel a cloud of smoke. "Even better."

David grinned. "I came to find my mother."

Dierdre made no effort to conceal her disappointment. "Your mother lives in Chicago?"

"Perhaps."

Dierdre leaned her elbows on the table, her chin resting on her clasped fingers, awaiting an explanation. A thin stream of smoke snaked up across her face.

"My mother abandoned my father and me when I was still a child. The last correspondence I received from her said that she had received an offer to perform in Chicago."

The waiter returned with steaming platters and heavy glass steins filled with dark lager.

Dierdre lifted her stein. "To the search for your mother."

David tipped his glass against hers.

"I confess that I had hoped your visit was really just pretense to see me again. I am disappointed to learn that you have another motive."

"I am sorry to disappoint you."

"You can still make it up to me," she replied. She cut into a medallion of veal. "Have you given any thought as to how you will find her?"

"Hopefully someone at a theater will remember her and know where she is. I had planned to telephone the local playhouses, but it hasn't proved as fruitful as I hoped. I may have to visit them all."

"This isn't Salt Lake City. There are scores of theaters."

"So I have discovered."

"You could well use the assistance of someone who knows their way around."

"Is that an offer?"

"Yes."

"It's a generous offer . . ."

"But . . ."

"But I feel I ought to do this alone."

Dierdre smiled defiantly. "It is just as well, David. All the longer I will have you in my city."

Just then, from outside the restaurant came a commotion. Across the street, two men engaged in fisticuffs over the contents of the restaurant's garbage can. Dierdre turned away.

"These incidents are becoming commonplace. These men act like wild animals."

"It is hunger."

"I shouldn't think they would be hungry. There are ample breadlines in the city."

"There are other ways to be hungry," David said. "Six weeks ago a truck delivering baked goods to the Drake was stopped near one of the breadlines and more than a thousand men mobbed the truck and made off with all the bread. Fortunately no one was hurt . . . except the bakery."

David turned back. "I hadn't heard that."

"It was in the *Sun.* After that the Drake insisted their vendors change their routes to avoid bread-lines and parks." She ground out her cigarette. "You know, Mary Pickford and Amelia Earhart have both stayed at the Drake. I am a great admirer of both."

"That does not surprise me."

"That they stay at the Drake or that I am an ad-mirer?"

"Neither surprises me. They are women like you, strong-willed and independent. Admirable qualities."

Dierdre blushed. "Thank you."

"In truth, I really do not know much about you. Except that you are quite different from your aunt."

"For which we are equally grateful. My family is fourth-generation Chicagoan. Back in the twenties, my father was mayor. He was, and still is, a very controversial figure. He did much to ease Prohibition's great thirsts, making him loved by some, hated by others, and distrusted by all. He is retired now, though he still keeps a hand in things—brings home an occasional governor or gangster."

"Governor or gangster?"

"Well, they both run the city." She smiled mischievously. "Actually there is not a great difference between the two, except the gangsters are much more amusing."

A smile spread across David's face. "And your mother?"

"Mother bides her time with crusades."

"What kind of crusades?"

"Oh, they change monthly. Mother chooses her causes with the same criteria that she selects her wardrobe."

Again, David smiled. "So what do you do?"

"The answer to that question is what keeps my father up at night. Vassar graduate, class of thirty-one. Now I just play, avoid marriage, and pretty much disappoint everyone." She lifted her glass to her chin. "And what does David Parkin do with his life?"

"Work. Though I also have a talent for disappointing."

"Aunt Victoria told me that you are a shrewd businessman."

"The truth be told, I am more lucky than shrewd. My father was a miner in Grass Valley, California. Thirteen years after my mother left we struck the mother lode. My father died two years later, and I ran the mine for a while before I sold it and moved to Salt Lake City to start the machinery company."

"It is better to be lucky than good."

"So I have heard."

"Why Salt Lake City?"

"My mother was going to meet me there. When I arrived she was gone."

"But you did meet your wife."

David's demeanor turned suddenly somber.

"I am sorry, I didn't mean to make you uncomfortable."

David wiped the corners of his mouth with his napkin. "Yes. That is where I met MaryAnne."

"My aunt told me some about her."

"Victoria never cared much for MaryAnne."

Dierdre sensed his agitation and quickly changed the topic, the conversation evolving to easy chatter. As the evening waned, David noticed Dierdre's necklace timepiece. It was a silver-cased pendant, its bevel inlaid with chips of diamonds and rubies.

"That is a beautiful timepiece."

"Are you bored of my company or are you really interested in timepieces?"

"You are easily the most candid woman I have ever met."

"Thank you. So which is it?"

"I collect timepieces. At least I used to. I'd hoard pretty much anything that kept time—even sundials."

She lifted it away from her breast. "My mother and father gave it to me for my graduation from college." She suddenly yawned, then laughed at herself. "It is late. You are probably exhausted. Are you ready to leave?"

"I am tired."

David laid down his napkin, and they both pushed back from the table. The ride back to the Drake was mostly silent. When the car stopped at the curb, Dierdre took David's hand.

"Thank you for dinner, David. I am very pleased that you are here."

"It was my pleasure."

She leaned over and kissed him on the cheek.

"As it was mine. May I see you again?"

The hotel's attendant opened the curb-side door and greeted David. David looked back.

"Perhaps we could have dinner again Tuesday evening?"

Dierdre beamed. "Swell. If you like we can have dinner at the Cape Cod Room inside the Drake. They have some of the best seafood in Chicago. You can update me on your search."

"I'll look forward to it." David stepped from the car to the pavement. "Good night, Dierdre. Thank you for your company."

"Good fortune finding your mother."

David smiled as he shut the door, bewildered that a woman as beautiful and sought after as she found him of such interest.

✦

The night Dierdre met David in the Saltair ballroom, she had felt something magnificent—the same intangible quality that MaryAnne and a thousand other women had instinctively felt in his presence. Included on that list was her aunt Victoria, who took perverse satisfaction in living vicariously through her niece's exploits.

Surrounded by the flux of society that pulsed through the Williamses' home, Dierdre had observed all types of men and found David a rare specimen. He was strong yet gentle, cunning yet harmless, rich yet unaffected by wealth's toxin.

MaryAnne presented no real concern to Dierdre, for while she did not care for the label "home wrecker," she ascribed no demonical significance to it either. Dierdre was accustomed to getting what she wanted, sometimes impeded by social mores and less frequently by conscience, but, in David's case, neither. His wife had deserted him and like a land title, when a claim is abandoned, it is open to the first to secure it. A mining man like David Parkin would understand that.

CHAPTER 14

A Second
Date

Will Rogers: "Now everybody has got a scheme to relieve unemployment. There is just one way to do it and that's for everybody to go to work. Where? Why, right where you are, look around and you will see a lot of things to do, weeds to cut, fences to be fixed, lawns to be mowed, filling stations to be robbed, gangsters to be catered to . . ."

FROM A NEWSPAPER
CLIPPING FOUND IN
DAVID PARKIN'S DIARY

Over the next three days, David's hunt for Rosalyn King proved fruitless, and David returned to his hotel room each night fighting mounting discouragement. He had experienced a brief glint of hope when a flamboyant, elderly actress at the Haymarket Theater recalled performing with Rose, and, with halting diction, divulged her fondest memories of the woman's exploits and her present situation and whereabouts. It was not until twenty minutes into her oration that David realized that the Rose she spoke of was a black woman from Kentucky. For the first time, he began to consider that his mother might never have really come to Chicago or, perhaps, had moved on as quickly as she came.

His lack of success also allowed time to think of MaryAnne, and the weight of her absence grew heavier with each passing day. Catherine had agreed to contact David at first word from MaryAnne, but he returned to his room each night with hope of that message only to be disappointed anew.

✦

Tuesday evening David met Dierdre in the Cape Cod Room—a small eatery annexed through a street-level corridor to the Drake Hotel. The restaurant was dark, mostly lit by the hurricane lanterns atop its red-checker-clothed tables. Their table was crowded with large platters of blushed spiny crab legs with glass dishes of butter, porcelain bowls of soup, and deep glasses of beer and juice. The bar was the restaurant's most prominent fixture, and it was always well-stocked, and occupied, and in its countertop were engraved the names of celebrities who had visited the establishment. And there were many.

Dierdre held her spoon out to him. "Try this."

"What is it?"

"Bookbinder soup. With a touch of sherry. It's a specialty here."

David sampled her offering. "That's good."

"I tried it without the sherry once. Didn't like it. Must be the southern girl in me."

"I have been meaning to ask you how a Chicago girl came to have a southern accent."

Dierdre stifled a laugh. She had worked hard to perfect her mother's southern drawl and deftly slipped in and out of it as benefited the situation.

"It is my mother's," she answered. "And, speaking of mothers, how goes the search for yours?"

"Twenty-one theaters, one job offer, and no one knows her."

"A job offer, that is impressive. I am a little hesitant to ask, but is it possible that your mother never settled in Chicago?"

"I am beginning to wonder."

Dierdre worked the meat from the crab leg's hollow with a crab fork. "You have come a long ways on faith."

"Faith or fate."

"You do not strike me as the fatalistic type."

"I am beginning to wonder. Are you a believer in fate?"

"You mean, like our chance encounter outside the ballroom?"

"That would count."

"Well, I don't believe in coincidence."

David wiped his mouth with a napkin. "A few days before MaryAnne left, she discovered a letter at our daughter's grave. It appears to be written by my mother. Catherine believes that it came at this time to lead me somewhere."

"Catherine, your housekeeper?"

"Right."

"It sounds very peculiar."

"I wonder."

"One thing I don't understand is why, after all this time, it is so important that you find her."

David looked at her thoughtfully. "I feel like I am trying to put together a puzzle of myself. To know why she left might help me understand who I am."

"Do you think she could answer that?"

"I don't know."

Dierdre set down her utensils. "May I ask you something very personal?"

David looked at her warily and his gaze made her reluctant.

". . . I would like to ask you about MaryAnne."

David turned the request over in his mind. "All right."

"Do you still love her?"

He hesitated. "She broke my heart when she left me."

Dierdre wondered if he had intentionally not answered her question. "Why did she leave?"

David stared listlessly at the lantern's candle as he deliberated on his response.

". . . If you would rather not talk about it."

David shook his head. "When our daughter died, I buried much of my heart with her." His voice wavered. "MaryAnne just grew tired of being alone."

"I don't mean to sound simplistic, but had you considered having more children?"

"We tried for years. But I couldn't give her children."

"Curious that you blame yourself. How do you know that she's not at fault?"

He paused, considering how much he desired to share. "Andrea wasn't really my daughter. Mary-Anne was pregnant with another man's child when I met her."

Dierdre tried to conceal her astonishment. "And still you married her?"

David nodded.

"David, that is the most beautiful thing I have ever heard."

David did not reply.

"Tell me about Andrea."

He smiled sadly. "She was joy. It was as though she healed everything in my life that was amiss."

"I bet you were a wonderful father."

David again grew quiet. Dierdre moved to change the subject.

"You mentioned that you collect clocks. I find that fascinating."

"I once had an extensive collection, but I've sold most of them now. I stopped collecting them after Andrea died. I collect other things now."

"What are you after these days?"

"Antiquities. Wooden boxes. Bibles."

"Bibles? How peculiar. Are you religious?"

"MaryAnne is quite pious, but I have never been accused of it."

Dierdre looked suddenly thoughtful. "Sometimes I wish that I were more religious. I frequently think about God, but I do not often attend church. I just want to go for the right reason—because I really believe it, not because it is socially advantageous." She suddenly grinned. "Of course that's another check on my father's blacklist."

"I think you are more religious than you give yourself credit for."

"How so?"

"There is integrity to your belief. I have to believe that pleases God."

"I don't think so. I think God wants blind observance."

"I find it difficult to accept that God created rational beings and would want them to be marionettes."

"Then what about faith?"

"Faith is misunderstood. It is treated as an end when, in fact, it is really a beginning."

"What do you mean?"

"It is a state we cultivate to get us somewhere—a principle of action. Every gold mine ever dug was dug by faith."

"But not all gold mines have gold."

"True, but you don't know that until you turn a shovel. It is only foolish, if one keeps panning when there is nothing there."

"I don't understand why faith is required at all. Why doesn't God just appear to everyone and tell them what He wants them to do?"

"Then we *would* become marionettes. We would do things because of the promise of reward or the threat of punishment, not because they are intrinsically good or noble. Our actions would change, but our hearts wouldn't. The truth is, in this life, cause and effect are often disjointed. Sometimes very bad things happen to very good people—sometimes for doing the right thing." At the statement David paused. ". . . like with Andrea."

"Still, there is too much confusion. I think it would make sense for God to appeal more to the senses."

"I have come to the conclusion that if the one universal truth of existence is the unknowing, then there must be something in the unknowing. I believe that's what life is about—to learn what it is about. And, to the level we apply ourselves to learning this, we evolve."

"Evolve to what?"

"Hopefully, to a state closer to God."

"How does religion fit into your theory?"

"It is part of that evolution. Religion, in a way, is like a clock. I used to have more than a hundred of them. I could tell you where every one of them came from, what company made them, sometimes even how. Yet, I am the first to admit that I do not comprehend time. The things that this German scientist, Einstein, talks about may only be the first real glimpse of our understanding of time." He lifted his pocket watch and unclasped the shell that protected its crystal. "But I can read a clock. In the same way I cannot comprehend God or the magnitude of power that could create an infinite universe, let alone the human mind. So if religion can help me to understand that being, then I am better off. As long as I do not confuse the clock for the time."

"That is profound, David."

"It just makes sense to me," David said. He yawned unexpectedly.

"Another long day?"

"They have all been long days. Or at least short nights."

"How about we call it an evening and have dinner again on Friday? If that's okay, I don't mean to distract you . . ."

David laughed. "You're a positive distraction. Our visits are the only things keeping me sane."

Dierdre's face animated. "Then why don't you

take tomorrow off and let me really show you the city. You could use the break."

David thought over the proposition.

"You have me for the day."

She smiled broadly. "Swell. I have some things I need to do in the morning. How about I come for you just before noon?"

David nodded. "I'll meet you at the curb." David signed the tab, then walked her out to the Duesenberg and a very patient Bennie.

❖

Back in Salt Lake City, the weather had again turned inclement. Large snowflakes fell and stuck to the roads. Traffic slowed. Children went inside their houses and waited for enough of it to fall to be of use. After the close of business, Gibbs knocked at the door of the Parkin house and was met by Catherine.

"Hello, Gibbs."

Gibbs removed his hat and tilted the snow off of it before brushing the snow from his shoulders and sleeves, then stepped inside the temperate foyer. "Catherine, have you heard from David recently?"

"Not a word since he left." She read the concern on his face. "Is something the matter?"

"Last night, there was a fire in the back lot of the building."

She raised a hand to her breast. "Oh my! Was anyone hurt?"

"No, and thankfully there wasn't damage to the building. The snow hindered it."

"Thank goodness."

"I wish that was all there was to it."

"What do you mean?"

"It wasn't an accident. The fire was started by a burning cross."

Catherine turned pale. "But why the machinery company?"

"Because David employs Negroes." A shadow of apprehension dimmed his countenance. "This isn't an isolated instance. I have read that some stores back East have been looted for doing the same."

"What are we going to do?"

Gibbs thought for a moment. "The police already know about it. There is nothing else to do." He replaced his hat and turned to leave. "If you hear from David, don't tell him. He already has enough on his mind."

CHAPTER 15

Riverview

"Dierdre is a woman endowed with the rare quality of contentment—the ability to find the joy possessed in each circumstance as mysteriously as the desert aborigine finds water in the parched desert . . ."

DAVID PARKIN'S DIARY.
JANUARY 11, 1934

Bennie stood at the Drake's front curbway, oblivious to the biting wind which funneled down the corridor of buildings, whistling through open doorways and alleys. When he saw David approach, he started for the rear passenger door and David quickly released him of the duty with an upraised hand and opened his door himself. Inside, Dierdre sat with her legs crossed and an open compact flat in one hand and a puff in the other. She was dressed in a long skirt and wore a thick mink coat. She looked up from the mirror.

"Good morning, David. I hope you brought a warm coat."

David pulled the door tight. "I brought my only coat. Where are we going?"

"That is a surprise."

She closed the compact, then examined his jacket. "I brought a blanket just in case."

As Bennie pulled away from the curb, David noticed the deferential glances of other drivers as they followed the car with covetous eyes. As they rounded the block, David asked Dierdre, "Have you ever driven this car?"

"My father won't let me. I would love to, though. The manufacturer claims it will go more than a hundred miles per hour. I would like to see if that is true."

Bennie glanced nervously into the rearview mirror.

"I am surprised," David said.

"That a Duesie can go that fast?"

"That your father can stop you from doing anything."

Dierdre laughed. "He has a little help. Watch," she whispered to David before leaning forward against the front seat.

"What do you say, Bennie? How about I drive today?"

Bennie's response was well rehearsed. "No, ma'am. I would lose my job. Your father gave me explicit instructions."

"You mean an explicit threat." She leaned in close. "He didn't say anything about David driving."

Bennie looked more anxious. "Please, ma'am. Your father would not like it."

She patted his shoulder gently, then leaned back into the seat. "Relax, Bennie. I am only kidding."

The extravagant automobile quietly moved forward, driving northward along the Chicago River until the terrain leveled to a broad area more than one hundred acres square. The wooden latticework peaks of roller-coasters rose above towering groves of sycamore and elm. As they neared the park, a large, circular sign read: RIVERVIEW AMUSEMENT PARK—JUST FOR FUN. Bennie pulled into the large, empty parking lot, drove up to the spacious front gate, and stopped the car.

"Riverview," announced Dierdre. "Home of two-ton Baker and the largest amusement park in the world."

David glanced around. "It looks to be the most unpopular amusement park in the world—that or it's closed."

Dierdre shuffled through the contents of her purse. "Of course it's closed, darling. It's winter."

Her reply produced more questions than it answered. Bennie opened Dierdre's door.

"We're here for a picnic," she said, and stepped out of the car. Bennie opened the car's trunk and brought out a straw picnic basket, which he handed to David. Bennie took his instructions from Dierdre, then returned to the car, and the automobile whisked away. David looked at the barred turnstiles beneath the large, twin-domed entrance and thought it looked a little like Saltair.

"How do we get in?"

"Through the front door."

She walked to the side of the turnstiles to a discreet door painted in the same rust pigment as the surrounding walls. She pushed it open to an austere, cement-bricked room. A doorway in the opposite wall entered into the park.

"It's the service entryway. The watchman is too lazy to come up front to let maintenance people in, so he just leaves it unlocked."

"How do you know that?"

She smiled. "I just do."

They walked out into the park, and at the entrance of the midway David stopped to take in the deserted landscape.

"Do you come here often?"

"During the summer I do. The boys always take me here. I think coming here makes them feel manly."

"How so?"

"It's the unwritten law of the sexes. I scream on the coasters, lose at skeeball, and wait excitedly as they spend two dollars assaulting innocent milk bottles to win a ten-cent stuffed animal for me. Not that I am averse to this. I think there is something very primal about it—like when cavemen dragged back a saber-toothed tiger to their women. Only they're throwing softballs, not spears." She gestured with one hand. "Who am I to flout evolution?"

"And so you play along."

"Of course." She smiled innocently. "I do want to show them a good time."

David started walking again. "Why are you revealing your secrets to me?"

"Because you are not a boy, and you see right through me."

She took his hand as they continued down the deserted midway towards the skeeball and the grotesque artwork of the freak shows.

She pointed to a large structure. "I love that ride. It's called the Flying Turns. It's a great ride." She suddenly chuckled. "I was on it once when my date pulled a Daniel Boone."

The phrase threw him. "A Daniel Boone?"

"Sorry. College jargon. It means that he shot his dinner."

David grinned. "Slang is the true line of demarcation between the generations."

"Are you saying that you are a lot older than me?"

"I am a lot older than you."

"Well, it's not like that's a bad thing. I like older men. At least I like you, and you're older." Somewhere a distant radio played "It's Only a Paper Moon," reminding David that they were not alone.

"The watchman's shanty is over there. But the codger never comes out," she said matter-of-factly. Dierdre reached into her bag and pulled out a box of cigarettes, offered one to David, who declined, then lit her own. A half mile into the park they stood across a row of boarded-up concessions.

"The summer before last, I had an interesting experience here. I was leaning against that rail eating an ice cream cone when this little waif of a boy came and stood in front of me, just watching me. Didn't say a thing. He just stood there looking like his eyes were going to pop out of his head. I asked him if he liked ice cream, and he nodded. So I bought him a cone and he ran off. A few minutes later this woman came up to me mad as a yellow jacket. She was dragging the little boy by one hand and holding the cone in the other. She said, 'What'ya think you're doin' buying him things his mama can't afford. How 'bout the other ones, huh?

What am I gonna tell the other ones?' The poor little boy just stood there sobbing his eyes out. She gave me the cone back and dragged the boy off. I just threw it away. What was I supposed to do with it? It was just an ice cream cone."

"To her it was self-respect. These are hard times. It's all most can do to hang on to their dignity."

"I still say it's just ice cream." She suddenly pointed east to a small parkway dotted with picnic tables beneath covered pavilions.

"There's the picnic grove."

They digressed off towards the hedged terrace.

"Does Salt Lake City have an amusement park?"

"Yes. In fact you have been to one of them. Saltair."

"Oh yeah. I noticed the roller-coaster. It wasn't very big for an amusement park."

"It's nothing like this. There's also a park called the Lagoon. It's twenty miles north of Salt Lake. It also has a roller-coaster."

"Riverview has seven."

She ground out her cigarette and threw it into the snow around the table. They sat down and Dierdre opened the basket.

"I brought grapes—in multiple incarnations." She brought out a cluster of Concord grapes and a bottle of wine, then reached back in and brought out a loaf of flatbread and cheese. She reached in once more. "And my favorite part of any meal— chocolate. Do you like chocolate?"

David nodded.

"I am addicted to it. My life has been much happier since I admitted that all I really want to eat is chocolate."

"I would say that it's hard on the body—but you couldn't tell by looking at you."

"Thank you. I was starting to wonder if you had noticed."

Dierdre broke apart the bread and spread a piece with cheese and handed it to David. David poured Dierdre a glass of wine, then held up the bottle.

"This is good wine."

"Good wine is all my mother would allow in the house."

He poured his own glass.

"Did you see the Ferris wheel?"

"Which one?"

"Doesn't matter. I was going to tell you that it was invented by the mayor of Chicago—George Ferris."

"I had heard something like that. It's fortunate that his last name wasn't Schmetzel. Somehow the Schmetzel wheel lacks romance."

Dierdre laughed. "What is your favorite amusement ride?"

"Probably the carousel."

She lit another cigarette. "Carousels are boring."

"There is not much to the ride, but there is something pleasant about the motion and the art of the menagerie. I have always been fond of carousels. They are a literal manifestation of peace—the turning of swords to plough-shares."

"Now that's an interesting take on an otherwise banal experience. Please explain yourself."

"Carousels were invented in the seventeenth century to train for jousting tournaments. French noblemen would mount barrels on a revolving platform and try to put their lances through hanging rings as they went around. Hence, the idiom 'to catch the brass ring.' Through time it evolved into a thing of pleasure and childhood—moving pieces of art."

"That's almost poetic."

"And you?"

"I like coasters. They say the Bobs is the fastest in the world, except for maybe the one at Coney Island. You a coaster fan?"

"Not much. I end up more dizzy than amused."

"Who doesn't?" She exhaled a careful stream of smoke through pursed lips. "The trick, David, is to enjoy the ride."

"And when the ride is over?"

She smiled. "You get back in line."

When they had finished eating, Dierdre stuffed everything back into the basket, laced her arm through its handles, and stood. "Let's go."

"Where are we off to now?"

She began to walk away. "The Tunnel of Love."

A hundred yards from the grove, the amusement came into view—a broad, flat facade, painted white with red hearts and cupids like an oversized valentine. The ride's boats were inverted and dry-docked to the side of the empty cement troughs that in the

open season held water. Dierdre set down the basket, and they both climbed over a short fence.

"This ride used to be called the Thousand Is-
lands. They changed the name to Tunnel of Love
and doubled their take. Image is everything."

"I have never walked through a Tunnel of Love."

She glanced towards the tunnel. "Me neither. But
I have paddled through it. A century ago, I dated
one of the owner's sons. When the ride is open, a
paddle wheel creates currents that take you through
the tunnels at its own pace, so lovers wanting to
spoon would sometimes climb off the boats in the
tunnel until an attendant came by and kicked them
out. This guy used to bring girls after hours, pull
out a canoe, and just paddle through. That way he
could stop wherever he wanted. He tipped the canoe over more than once."

"With you in it?"

She smiled and did not answer. Suddenly, a barrel-chested man wearing the top half of a navy-blue
uniform appeared outside the gate. On his chest
was the shield of the Riverview Police. His face
was florid. "Hey. What are you doing in there?"

They both looked over.

"I'll talk to him," David said. Dierdre smiled
helplessly as David climbed over the fence and began talking to the man, who grew only more vehement as the discussion progressed. After a few
minutes, Dierdre calmly approached. She put her
hand on David's shoulder.

"Just a minute, David," she said, gesturing for

him to step back. She turned towards the watch-man, and though David could not hear what she said, the man's demeanor quickly changed from rage to impotence. He turned and sauntered away.

"What did you say to him?"

"Like I said, I dated the owner's son. C'mon."

They climbed back over the fence.

"You are used to getting your way."

"What do you mean by that?"

"It was just an observation."

"I was born into a wealthy and prominent family. I can't help that. But I don't flaunt it, and I don't abuse it. It is important to me to make it on my own."

"I didn't mean to imply otherwise."

David slid down into the concrete trough, then held up his hand to Dierdre, who took it, then slid down next to him.

"The truth is, I can never truly be fully independent, because I know there is always a safety net. Like that guard incident. I was curious to see how you handled him, but I knew in the end that we would get our way. It's debilitating in a way."

"It's just the way it is."

"Maybe that's why I find you so interesting."

"Why is that?"

"You're not a sure thing."

They walked on through the empty troughs into the tunnel and beyond until Dierdre complained of being cold, and David lay the blanket across her shoulders.

"What time will Bennie return?"

"Oh, he's been parked out front for hours. He only left because I had a few errands for him in the city."

"What does he do when he's out there?"

"Just reads, I think. Though he's more likely to read Captain Whizbang than Hemingway. He says he likes it. People would die for his job."

"People would die for any job."

"A while back we almost had to let him go."

"Why?"

"You know, the Negro thing—coloreds taking good jobs while white men are out of work. My father was getting hassled by some of his colleagues. He usually succumbs to such things, but he drew the line at Bennie."

"That's commendable."

"Oh, he's hardly noble. It's just that good chauffeurs are hard to find." Her face suddenly brightened. "Would you like to see the house? I could fix dinner."

"Sounds unusually domestic."

"I can be domestic."

On their way out of the park, David caught sight of the shamed watchman as he darted behind a structure to avoid further humiliation.

※

The Williamses resided in the Lake Forest district of Chicago, not far from the Drake or the street

called Millionaires' Row. At their arrival, the Duesenberg passed between two brick pilasters topped
with cement platforms which supported brass cupids, their arms extended to hold aloft electric
globes. The Williams's mansion was not set back
far from the street, but was well secluded by trees
and foliage—an arboretum of red oak, red maple,
elm, beech, and cottonwood. As they cleared the
landscape, the mansion came into view. It was a
large, three-story structure, surrounded on all sides
by groves of trees. Its facade was blanketed by ivy
with ocher-hued stucco exposed in rare patches.

"Have you lived here long?"

"Always."

"It is beautiful," he noted.

Bennie stopped the car at the side of the house
and attended to their doors. As they entered the
home, they were met by a handsome woman with
greying hair and almond-shaped eyes climaxed by
dark, swooping eyebrows. She appeared to be not
much older than David, who, without introduction,
immediately knew who she was for, though much
more svelte, she showed a remarkable resemblance
to her sister Victoria. The woman eyed David
furtively.

"Dierdre, I thought you were out for the evening,"
she said with a prominent southern drawl.

"Hello, Mother. I wanted to show my friend our
home." She turned to David. "This is David Parkin.
He is the man I met in Salt Lake City. He is a friend
of Aunt Victoria's."

Her expression relaxed, and she gracefully extended her hand. "It is a pleasure, Mr. Parkin. I am Samantha. Dierdre has spoken of you."

David noticed Dierdre's blush.

"It is my pleasure, ma'am."

"You came all this way to see our Dierdre?"

"Actually, I was in town on other matters, and we happened to run into each other at the Drake Hotel."

"What an odd coincidence," she said, raising her eyebrows. "All the same it is a pleasure having you in our home."

"Thank you."

"Will you be staying for dinner?"

Dierdre interjected. "I told David that I would fix him something."

"Nonsense, Dierdre, you'll poison the man. We will be dining in a half hour. I'll have Claire lay a few more settings. Why don't you all just retire to the billiards room until we are called?"

Dierdre relented, though she was clearly annoyed by her mother's insistence on interfering with her evening.

"Come, David."

✦

The bricked patio was visible from the spacious room, encircled by the garden and a pond lined by a wrought iron fence and weathered garden statuary. Dierdre walked up beside him.

"Most of my parents' social functions are held out on the patio. There used to be swans."

"What happened to them?"

"My mother was hosting a campaign fund raiser for an alderman and was standing by the pond when one of the birds took after her. You wouldn't think a woman could move so quickly in a long gown and heels. The bird only stopped chase when one of the guests headed it off with a pair of salad tongs. Everyone who is anyone was there, and to my mother's mortification, at every social function since then someone has recalled the incident."

David laughed. "What became of the swan?"

"Mother would have had the thing roasted if my father had allowed it. He sent them off to a park somewhere in the city. Mean birds, swans. Beautiful things are often mean."

Outside the room a bell rang.

"That would be dinner," Dierdre drawled unenthusiastically.

      ✦

The oak-paneled dining room was immense, yet so garishly lavished with bric-a-brac as to render the room cramped. The three of them sat down to one end of an elongated table, with Samantha at the head and Dierdre across from David. A servant came to David's side with a platter.

"Do you like mutton, David?" Samantha asked.

"Mutton? Yes. Very much."

The servant forked a piece of meat on his plate. "Not everyone cares for mutton."

Dierdre said, "Personally, I prefer swan."

Samantha glared at Dierdre, then turned back towards David.

"How long have you known Victoria?"

"Since I moved to the Salt Lake Valley."

"Then you are not a native."

"No. I was born in a small mining town in northern California. I moved to Salt Lake City around the turn of the century. I met Victoria shortly after my arrival—at some affair."

"That is where one would meet Victoria. Frankly, I am surprised that she ever allowed her husband to locate in the West. But business is business, I suppose. I was sure she would come back after his death, but she hasn't. My theory is she likes to complain about living there, and if she moved she would have nothing to whine about."

David smiled knowingly. "You underestimate her ability to whine."

Samantha laughed heartily, covering her mouth with a linen napkin. "You do know her well." She lowered the cloth. "Personally, I find your city charming. The mountains are spectacular. I was there once in the fall, and the autumn leaves made the mountains look like an artist's drop cloth."

"It is beautiful." He took a fork of baked sweet potato, followed with a drink. "Dierdre tells me that you are involved in many causes."

"It is how I bide my time. Seems there is always

something." She daintily raised a spoon of soup to her mouth, sipped it, then just as delicately returned it to the dish. She suddenly asked, "Are you wealthy?" She asked the question with the candor one might have used to inquire of one's health. Dierdre glared at her.

"I have sufficient means," David said.

"I find it hard to believe that a man of your looks and station has not yet married."

Dierdre interjected. "David *was* married, Mother."

David wasn't sure which comment he found more disturbing. He had no idea how to respond to either.

"You are a widower?" Samantha asked.

David looked embarrassed. "No. My wife left me."

There was an uncomfortable silence, and Dierdre again glared at her mother.

When they had finished their entrées Dierdre looked down at her watch. "I better get David back to his hotel."

"It is getting late," David said. He set his napkin on the table. "Thank you for dinner."

Samantha stood. "It was a pleasure having you in our home, Mr. Parkin. Victoria is fortunate to have such handsome friends."

Dierdre walked to the doorway and hollered for Bennie, then returned to escort David out to the car. When they were out of the drive, Dierdre said, "I thought we would never get out of there. My mother liked you."

"How could you tell?"

"If she stays in the room long enough to learn your name she's intrigued. The dinner invitation was unprecedented."

"Maybe it is because I am nearly her age."

"Bennie is nearly her age."

The chauffeur glanced up in the mirror.

"Maybe it's because you are handsome." David wondered if she was jealous of her own mother. Dierdre leaned into David's shoulder. He lifted his arm and put it around her. A half hour later they stopped in front of the hotel.

"It was a wonderful day," Dierdre said in a lilting voice. "Even with my mother's contribution. Thank you for sharing it with me."

"It was nice to escape."

"Sometimes it's necessary to escape." She sighed. "I do have one regret . . . Besides my mother."

"Oh?"

"The Tunnel of Love was a perfectly good waste of dark," she said playfully. "Are we still on for Friday?"

"Seven o'clock?"

"Swell."

There was another lull, and Dierdre looked away. Finally she said, "This is where you kiss me good night, David."

David grinned sheepishly, then pensively leaned forward to kiss her. A broad smile blanketed her face.

"Night night, sweetie."

"Good night, Dierdre." David stepped out of the car, and Bennie shut the door behind him.

"Good evening, sir."

"Good night, Bennie."

David stood at the curb as the Duesenberg slowly pulled away. Something inside of him ached. Since he had married, MaryAnne was the only woman he had ever kissed.

✦

"This world ain't going to be saved by nobody's scheme. It's fellows with schemes that got us into this mess. Plans can get you into things but you got to work your way out."

WILL ROGERS

✦

Early Friday morning, Dierdre knocked on the door of David's hotel room unannounced. When he finally answered, he wore only a robe, his hair was tousled, and his face, partially concealed beneath a shadow of unshaven stubble, still held the creases of his aborted slumber.

"Good morning, sunshine," she said brightly.

"I thought you meant seven P.M."

"I did. I'm just twelve hours early."

She stalked past him into the room, dressed in a bright print with matching shoes, the ensemble capped by a light green turban, as effervescent as the colors she wore beneath. She systematically set about opening the room's blinds while David watched drowsily.

"You look adorable, all rumpled and unshaven."

"You are fairly glowing. What is Chicago's most refulgent debutante doing out at this hour?"

"I am a woman on a mission." She glanced around the room. "Do you have coffee?"

"Not yet."

"Here. I brought you something." She walked over and handed him a single sheet of paper.

David glanced at it curiously. "Another listing of theaters?"

"Not just any old listing."

He sat down on the sitting room couch to examine the sheet. He noticed a date printed in its text. It read 1902.

"This listing is old."

"Ancient. You will notice that I marked a particular theater. The Gaiety."

The theater's name had been circled in ink.

"What is significant about the Gaiety?"

Dierdre sat down next to him, pausing for emphasis. "It is the theater where your mother performed."

David's face animated from disbelief to excitement. "You found her?"

"I told you that I have connections. An actor friend of mine found her. Congratulations, David, your mother really was here."

"Dierdre, thank you." He put his arms around her.

Dierdre felt rhapsodic in his embrace, and her face moved closer to his, brushing up against his rough cheek. She suddenly pressed her lips against his, then put her hands behind his head and pulled his face tighter against hers, moving her body into his. Her turban fell off with the motion. To her surprise, David suddenly pulled back.

"No."

Her eyes flashed an emotion somewhere between bewilderment and anger.

"What is wrong?!"

"I am still married."

His reason enraged her. "Perhaps you should inform your wife, wherever she is, because she seems to have forgotten."

". . . and I still love her."

Dierdre took up her turban, stood, then brushed down her dress. She exhaled slowly, and her voice softened.

"I'm sorry. I'm just frustrated. Your wife didn't even have the civility to tell you that she was leaving you. I don't see why she should deserve such devotion and I such pain."

"She's still my wife. A deal's a deal."

"She reneged on the deal."

"It is my fault that MaryAnne left. I am not ready to give her up." He looked down. "No matter how attracted I am to you."

His confession surprised both of them. Dierdre walked to the door and opened it. "I admire your loyalty almost as much as I despise it. We felt something, David. Something real."

When the door closed, David shook his head and sighed. After a while he lifted Dierdre's list and looked again at the denoted theater. Somewhere through the years his mother's existence had developed a mythlike quality, and now seeing the theater where she had actually performed filled him with a strange sensation. The Gaiety Theater.

Still unshaven and unkempt, David quickly dressed and descended to the lobby. He returned to the concierge's counter. Despite his appearance, the concierge recognized him from before. "How goes the hunt?"

"I have a theater name, but it is not listed in the directory that you gave me."

"The phone directory is the most current city listing available. What is the name of your theater?"

"The Gaiety." David held up the outdated listing. "It is an older theater."

He examined the list, then returned it.

"Some of these smaller theaters change names and ownerships nearly as often as their productions. Your theater is probably long gone."

David groaned. "Then I am back to where I started."

"I am sorry, sir. I would be happy to check with a few managers of some of the older theaters to see if they know anything about the Gaiety."

"That would be helpful."

"If I find something I will leave a message in your room."

Disheartened, David thanked him, then stepped away from the counter. Just then a young bell captain, corpulent and ruddy-faced, tapped him on the shoulder.

"Excuse me, sir, but I overheard you speaking of the Gaiety Theater."

"Yes. I am looking for it."

"I know a man who worked at the Gaiety. Up until they shut it down."

"Do you know Rose King?"

"I don't know anything about the place except this guy. He worked in the Drake's kitchen for a couple weeks. But he was always stinko. They caught him filching from the liquor shelf and fired him."

"Do you know where I would find him?"

"I still run into him every now and then out front of the hotel. He walks past here to get to an old gin mill about a mile from here. It's called Barleys, or something like that. It's a grey, cinder-block building with no windows, just a door—right across the street from the Rookery on LaSalle."

"What is your friend's name?"

"Fellow's name is Hill. Hill Simons. I don't know how much good he'll be to you. You can bet he'll be loaded for bear."

David handed him a bill. "You don't know how helpful you've been."

The young man pocketed the paper.

"I don't recommend you go down there after

dark. It's down near a hobo jungle they call the Hoover Hotel. They'll roll a man down there for a plug nickel."

"Thanks for the tip."

"Anytime, sir." He patted his trouser pocket. "Thank you for yours."

CHAPTER 16

John Barleycorn's Tavern

"It is folly of our species that we reserve the greatest bouquets for our dead."

DAVID PARKIN'S DIARY.
JANUARY 12, 1934

The grey, windowless tavern was nearly as obscure as it was during Prohibition when it was a blind pig, its bootlegging concealed behind the sedate facade of a tobacco shop. Only a crudely hand-painted sign that read JOHN BARLEYCORN'S TAVERN betrayed its locale. A cab released David at the sidewalk fronting the bar, and he walked uneasily into the building, barely acknowledged by the dozen or so denizens who were scattered throughout. The main room was dim and smoke-filled, lit by the weak, yellow incandescence of low-wattage globes and the ocher glow of cigarettes. A barrel-chested, aproned barkeep stood behind a counter polishing a glass with a grey and threadbare dishcloth. A smoldering cigar dangled from one side of his mouth.

"I am looking for Hill Simons."

The barkeep continued his motion as his eyes scrutinized the disheveled newcomer.

"You got money?"

"I do."

He gestured with a toss of his head. "Over there."

At a round table in the corner of the room sat the man—elfish in stature and feature, his bald head framed from rear to temple by tenacious sprigs of hair and long sideburns that fell to his sharp jaw in a scraggly mass. He wore a soiled green shirt and denim jeans, his attire matching his persona—disheveled and sloven. He suckled the rim of an empty glass as he stared blankly ahead. The table was bedecked with several other glass mugs and bottles, all drained except for the foam.

David approached the table.

"Hill Simons?"

The elf looked at him suspiciously, his glassy eyes tinged in the florid markings of inebriation. His mouth was covered by the upper rim of the glass.

"I don't know you," he said flatly, the words echoing in the glass he spoke into.

"I am looking for a woman named Rosalyn King. I was told that you might know where she is."

"Where she is?" he chuckled with a drunken laugh. "Feedin' fish."

David squinted at the cryptic reply, then extended his hand. "David Parkin."

The man made no effort to reciprocate. David lowered his hand.

"What interest you got in Rosie?"

"It's personal."

A smirk crossed the man's face. "Not likely to be professional . . . 'less she owed you money. What kind of personal?"

"My personal," David replied tersely.

The man grunted and turned back to his empty glass, still mourning its demise. "Your personal ain't worth my time."

David looked at the table strewn with dead soldiers, then took two bills from his vest and waved them beneath the man's nose. The man's quick eyes darted back and forth between David and his bribe.

"I will buy drinks as you talk."

The man cautiously reached up and, at David's nod, slipped the bills from his hand. Money pressed in his fist, he raised his hand to the bartender, who turned back to a wooden casket and filled a glass mug. The man looked decidedly relieved. "What you want to know about Rosie? I know it all."

"How did you know her?"

"I was working gas at a burlesque show on the lakeside with her. The Folly. Mostly hoofers. Not much talent but lots of shaking." He smiled weakly. "Folly went out least fifteen years before the Gaiety. Though it never really was in business—not the moneymaking kind. When it went under Rosie swapped to the Gaiety."

"I've never heard of the Folly."

"It ain't around no more. That's how these things are. Life span of a tsetse fly."

"Where do you work now?"

He chortled. "This here's my job. Help 'em clean out their bottles. Haven't worked theater for years."

"Why?"

"What's that got to do with Rosie?"

"Nothing. Just curious."

He wiped at his nose. "Innovations. What's a gas man got to do when there's electric lights?"

"Were you close to Rose?"

"With Rose? Nah. Nobody got close with Rosie. More thorn than flower to that one."

"How do you know so much about her?"

"Hang 'round Rosie long enough, and you'd hear it all—whether you want to or not. Woman was a walking ballad. Though I never suspected much of it was true."

"What was true?"

"Her stories . . . claimed she was the penniless widow of a millionaire gold miner someplace out West in California. Hit it big just after she divorced him. And, there's the boy she left behind and was always cryin' about. Way I see it, if the woman walked, then she ain't got no claim on none of it anyhow. But like I said, don't suspect any of it was true. No one did. Woman just wasn't singing from a full hymnal."

"Both of you came over from the Folly?"

"Yeah, but not at first. When the Folly went under she left town. Said she was going back to her man in Californy. Truth was she was past her prime, and she knew it. Then she came back a month later with a boatload of money. Crazy amount, more than twenty thousand dollars I heard. Told everyone her son gave her the jake. Some said it proved her story about the millionaire husband, but I didn't give it much credence. She probably put the bite on some fool politician or something. Rose was always catchin' trouble with high-hats. Had the right bait for it."

"What did she do after she got the money?"

"When she was out West she met a guy named Adam Mason. Mason was a has-been stage producer turned charlatan. His ruse was that he was gonna make Rose a big star in his new production. After she was all excited, Mason just happened to lose his financing. He was smooth all right. Real oil merchant. Rosie thought it was her own idea to invest her money in the show. The day she relinquished the jake, Mason run off with two calico skirts and Rosie's last nickel."

David grimaced.

"Just the way it goes in this business. Woman wanted too much too bad, and the devil took her soul without ever deliverin' the goods."

"Then what happened to her?"

"Went on the skids. Next time I saw her she looked to have drunk on fifty pounds or more." He looked at his glass as if talking about her drinking had made him thirsty. "Funny thing, her voice wasn't that bad after that." The man pointed to his throat. "Fat improves the vocals. Just like all those bohunk opera singers. Fat, all of 'em."

"What happened to her?"

"She got her break. They gave her a billing at the Gaiety. Poor Rose," he lamented, shaking his head in mock sympathy. "Ship finally came in, and it sank in the harbor. Show stunk. The Gaiety was already hanging by a prayer. Place went belly-up. Papers blamed it on Rose cuz it was her name on the marquee. Said she had the kind of talent that could darken a stage permanently. Rosie couldn't buy a job after that. She was too fat for the burlesque. So she dropped her own curtain."

"Dropped her curtain?"

The man ran a finger across his throat. "Croaked herself."

David stepped back as if he had received an electrical shock.

"She is dead?"

"More than ten years cold." He gestured with a shaky hand. "It's practically lore. She jumped from a bridge the day they chained the theater doors." An anemic smile crossed his face. "There's a limerick about it. It's kind of catchy."

He spat into one of the drained glasses.

". . . 'once was a woman named King, Who feigned had the talent to sing, But the crowds disagreed, and her failure decreed, So King, from a bridge, took a fling.'"

David just stared at the man.

"She left a letter at the theater tellin' them she was gonna jump. It made all the papers. Not that anyone would remember. Wasn't exactly front page news." He grinned noxiously. "'ronic, ain't it? She wanted to be famous and finally got it. Just wasn't around to enjoy it." He took a drink. ". . . or whatever you do with fame."

David's rage rose against the little man. The man sensed his growing hostility.

"What's this Rose to you?"

"Where's the letter?"

"The theater's new owners got it. Cuthbert and Sinclair. Cuthbert was there when it was found."

"Where do I find this theater?"

"Six, seven miles from here. Down off Burley. It's not the Gaiety no more. It's the Thalia."

David threw a final bill on the table and turned to leave. The man smiled and raised his mug. "Thanks for the sap, sport."

As David walked out of the tavern the elf hailed another round.

CHAPTER 17

The Gaiety

*"There is no more constant companion
than the specter of regret."*

DAVID PARKIN'S DIARY.
JANUARY 12, 1934

The day the Gaiety Theater closed, the Chicago tabloids eulogized its demise with such eloquent and strident prose that one would never suspect their contribution to its murder—poisoning it with malicious ink. The paper had proclaimed the theater company's swan song, a pirated performance of Gilbert & Sullivan's *H.M.S. Pinafore,* as "the worst tragedy in Chicago theater since the Iroquois Theatre fire."

Like the Iroquois Theatre, the Gaiety's stage was darkened. The bankers added their own toxic ink to the title's default, and the theater's pulse ceased. The marquee was stripped, doors locked and boarded, while Rosalyn King observed in silence as her name fell from the marquee to a jumbled pile of wooden letters, then hobbled twelve blocks to her residence in the lightless tenement houses of Whiskey Row. In the damp, hopeless confines of the tenement, she wrote three letters, left two on the tobacco-stained counter where she had penned them, then, an hour past dusk, slid the third beneath the door of the now vacant theater, and was never heard from again.

The letter, like the theater, was unopened for nearly a decade, until new money breathed life into its vacant halls and galleries. The deed was trans-

ferred, carpets pulled up, and the gas lamps replaced by incandescent globes. The lobby, once
embellished with gaudy, faux Raphaels, had been
overpainted in the streamlined graphics of the art
deco style, which was popular at that time. It was
during the theater's resurrection that Rose's letter
was discovered by a laborer, who immediately
surrendered it to his employer—Theodore Cuthbert III.

The entrance to the Thalia was obstructed by an
iron-caged ticket window, shadowed beneath a
large marquee that protruded out over the sidewalk,
arrayed with large, gilt letters, and a flashing bor-
der of electric globes. The outer doors were unlocked, and David entered, glancing around the
empty lobby for any indication of occupancy.

The walls and carpeting were cardinal red, and
large murals were aligned along the back walls,
framed in English walnut borders. To the left of the
concessions was a narrow, red door with the word
"Office" engraved on a brass plate. David knocked
on the door, then, finding it unlocked, twisted the
knob and entered.

The room was occupied by the theater's owners:
Theodore Cuthbert and Alma F. Sinclair. A rotund,
aging gentleman with receding, grey hair sat at a
pine writing table cluttered with more trash than
the receptacle that lay next to it. His wooden chair,
as his demeanor, was casually reclined. The other
man, only a few years his junior, was lanky and of
autumn complexion. He leaned against the back

paneled wall, his umber hair concealed beneath the bowl of a derby. They both took the intruder to be a vagabond.

David guessed at the identity of the seated man. "Mr. Sinclair?"

Surprised to hear his name, the standing man responded. "You have the advantage, sir. I am Sinclair."

"My name is David Parkin. I was told that you are in possession of a letter left by a woman who once performed at this theater. Rosalyn King."

"You a newspaper man?"

"No."

"Newspapers want to see that letter from time to time," said Sinclair.

"Why?"

The seated man spoke. "The legend, of course."

"I don't know anything about a legend."

"Why, then, are you here?" Cuthbert asked with obvious annoyance.

"I was hoping to see the letter."

The husky man leaned forward. "Regrettably, we haven't the time to satisfy every curiosity seeker who lands in here off the street. But if you would like to buy a ticket to tonight's performance, we will gladly see to it."

David stood dormant. He looked at the two men for a moment, then said softly, "I have greater interest in the letter than mere curiosity. Rosalyn King was my mother."

His words seemed to hang in the air, affecting the

men with a gravity David could not have anticipated. The two men exchanged glances of astonishment.

"You are Rose King's son?" Sinclair asked.

"King was my mother's maiden name. Her stage
name as well. She abandoned my father and me."

"Good Lord, it is just like the letter!" Cuthbert
gasped.

"I would like to see the letter," David repeated.

"We have it locked away in the vault," Cuthbert
said. "It is valuable."

". . . valuable?"

"The business that has been generated from that
one letter probably accounts for a quarter of our
take. Maybe more," Sinclair said.

Cuthbert leaned forward. "A little more than
twenty years ago, for one week, your mother was
the star performer here. Her show failed and the
theater with it. The theater used to be called the
Gaiety. It was teetering on the brink of financial
ruin for several years, in fact, nothing short of a
miracle would have saved it. But Rose was blamed
for the failure. The day they closed the house, your
mother slid a letter between the front doors. Just
before she took her life. When we purchased the
theater back in eighteen, a worker found the letter
on the lobby floor. I was there at the time and witnessed its opening."

Sinclair stood from the wall. "There were actually three letters. We possess only one of them. One
was written to her landlady. The other, presumably,

was for you. She lived in a tenement a mile or two from here, down on Whiskey Row. Her landlady brought them by, thinking she could get us to pay some of Rose's old debts. Seems her rent was in arrears. Everyone's is these days, but back then it was criminal."

"What of this legend? And what does my mother's letter have to do with it?"

"Your mother . . ." Sinclair paused to glance over to Cuthbert, as if seeking his approval to proceed. ". . . your mother is considered, by some, to be a ghost."

David looked at Sinclair incredulously. He continued. "The letter was a suicide note. She cursed the previous owners and wrote about haunting them."

David's face stiffened. "Haunting?"

". . . and she mentioned you," Cuthbert added.

"What did she say of me?"

"She spoke of your return. In fact there has been verse written about it."

"I've heard the limerick."

Cuthbert pulled on his fingers until the joints popped. ". . . 'so King, from a bridge, took a fling.' That is not the one I was referring to. There is another."

"I didn't know."

"There is a ritual that occurs before each performance," Sinclair interjected. "It is followed religiously. The performers gather around a vase and drop in a coin. Then they chant, 'A penny for

Rose—a prayer for her son—that the take may be vast—and her child will come.'"

David did not respond but looked down thoughtfully. The partners joined his solitude.

"And I came."

"Yes you did." Cuthbert rubbed his chin. "Yes, you certainly did. I am not the superstitious type, mind you, but I do find this all rather odd."

David was unsure of what to think. It was certainly not the end he believed he would meet. "Does my mother haunt the halls?"

"If there is an apparition, I have never seen it," said Sinclair. "Though it is no surprise to me that they imagine the thing. These are thespians. They fancy a shadow into a phantom."

"They also believe the world will someday throw daisies at their feet," Cuthbert mocked. "You tell me which is more likely."

"May I see the letter?"

Cuthbert took from his desk's side drawer a key attached to a heavy brass ring and tossed it to his partner. Sinclair left the office, then returned a moment later with the letter and handed it to David. David extracted the well-creased parchment from the envelope and carefully unfolded the paper. The scrawl looked similar to that in the letters he had scrutinized in his den.

✦

March 17, 1912
To the proprietors of the Gaiety.
Messrs.
With the closure of the Gaiety, you have effectively ended my career, as my life, for they are the same. Tonight, I shall throw myself from the Troop Street bridge. May my demise haunt your despicable lives and the curtain fall on all of your ambitions, as they have mine. I regret having been enslaved by the bonds of my ambitions. But I confess a greater regret, that I mistook this pantomime for something real—a life that might have brought lasting joy instead of the vaporous illusion of fame and fortune. My husband died in my absence. I have not seen my son since he was but six. I once fantasized that one day he would come to the theater to see me perform, and that our reunion would be grand. I am now certain that he should only know the bitterness of betrayal. Adieu.

ROSALYN KING

✦

There ensued a moment of thoughtful solitude. Finally Cuthbert cleared his throat. "Gaston Leroux has made the haunted theater of popular consequence, as well as financial. I do not suppose that we shall tell anyone of your appearance. You are much more useful as lore."

"No," David replied stoically. "I don't suppose you will."

"Are you staying in town?"

"At the Drake Hotel."

The men were surprised at the answer, as his state of dishevelment would not even qualify him as kitchen help at the luxurious inn.

"Then we may surmise that you are affluent," Sinclair said.

David nodded matter-of-factly. Cuthbert drew out several printed passes, offering them to David. "If you would please, they are vouchers for tonight's show."

David accepted the tickets.

"May I walk through your theater? I would like to see where my mother once performed."

"As you please. It has all been refurbished since she was here, but the main stage and fascia are principally the same. Take as much time as you wish. You can leave the way you entered."

"Thank you."

David left the men's company and entered the theater beneath the overhang of a balcony which shadowed a third of the main floor and, at each side of the auditorium, protruded in a single thrust of stepped, box seats. The floor gradually declined to a modest-sized, elliptical stage, its foot dressed in jet-black fabric. Massive red curtains, gold-ribbed and fringed, were pulled open and gathered to the stage's extremities, tied back in great, gilt ropes. Gold-leafed statues of demon-faced Greek gods and nymphs were carved into the large arch facade that encircled the stage. The stage was occupied with the sets and props of the current production— a southern scene with white picket fences and facades of homes propped up by obscured wooden beams.

He scanned the room, advanced slowly to the stage's perimeter, climbed the dais, then walked out to center stage, where his mother had once performed. The floorboards groaned beneath him, and each step confessed the platform's longevity. From the back of the stage, he heard the gentle fall of footsteps. David followed the sound, stepping to the side of the bound curtain into the shadow of the wings. He suddenly shook his head in wry amusement. At his feet lay an earthen jar nearly filled to its brim with copper pennies. More footfalls. He took a deep breath and looked around the dark, seemingly vacant stage back. To his own surprise, he suddenly whispered in a hushed, forced voice, "Mother?" He took a few more steps in the direction of the footfalls. "Mother?"

"Mr. Parkin?"

David spun to his side. Cuthbert stood alone at the backstage doorway wearing a perplexed countenance.

"I am sorry if I startled you. I thought this would be of interest to you."

He handed David a torn piece of paper with an address scrawled across it.

"It is the address of the tenement house where your mother boarded. It is about a dozen blocks north, just over the Troop Street bridge she jumped from. I don't know if they are still standing, but I suspect they are. Cost more to demolish them than they are worth."

"Thank you. Do these doors exit to the street?"

"Out to Fifty-third."

David folded the paper into his pocket and left the building. He walked nearly a mile before he remembered the night's engagement and hailed a cab back to the hotel to meet Dierdre for dinner. He had no idea whether she would come or not, but after the morning's incident he expected to be dining alone.

CHAPTER 18

Dierdre's
Proposition

*"Still no word from MaryAnne.
My feelings cannot be far distant from those
of the dustbowl farmer who, looking out over
his withered fields to the blanched sky above,
wonders why it will not rain."*

DAVID PARKIN'S DIARY.
JANUARY 11, 1934

At ten minutes past the top of the hour, Dierdre sauntered into the dining room followed, as usual, by the ardent gaze of the waiters and male patrons and the indignant or envious gazes of the womenfolk. She was dressed casually in a pleated salmon crepe skirt with a cap of matching fabric. She wore a sheer silk blouse. David rose and pulled back her chair.

"I'm sorry I'm late," she said, smiling sheepishly.

"You look very nice," David said.

"It is a little daring. I thought that you might like it." Her smile receded. "Thank you for being here. I need to say this first. I want to apologize for this morning."

"There is no need."

"Yes there is. I had no right to be angry. There should be more men like you. I just wished it was me you were loyal to."

David smiled, but had no idea what to say.

"Did the lead I brought you help?"

David nodded, and Dierdre's face animated in genuine excitement.

"You found your mother?"

"In a sense." His voice lowered. "My mother is dead. She committed suicide twenty-two years ago."

Dierdre covered her mouth. "Oh, David. I am so sorry."

"I cannot believe that I have come all this way to leave without answers."

His words filled her with dread.

"Then you will be leaving soon?"

"Not until the day after tomorrow. I still need to visit the tenement house she once lived in. I was told that she left a letter for me there."

Her demeanor grew more somber. "I will be sorry to see you go," she said softly. Neither spoke for a moment. "David. Remember the other day, when you asked me if I believed in fate?"

He nodded.

"I believe that you were meant to come to Chicago. But not necessarily for the reasons you think." She looked at him seriously. "These last few days have been very special. I have learned a lot about myself and life that I didn't know before. I have experienced feelings that are new to me. There is an inexplicable chemistry between us."

David gazed at her intently.

"What is left for you in Salt Lake City but pain?"

"My home."

"This would be a better home. We belong together, David. We would be very happy." She smiled. "We would be the toast of society. The Fitzgeralds of Chicago—Scott and Zelda. It would be a magnificent life we would share. And I would be proud to be seen on your arm." She took his hand. "I know this is a confusing time. But you care for me, David. And I care deeply for you. There is nothing complicated about that."

David looked down.

"Please tell me that you care for me."

David said nothing, and Dierdre's eyes began to moisten.

"Then tell me that you don't. Tell me that you have no feelings for me, and I will leave you alone."

Again David could not respond.

She touched the corner of her eye. "You do have feelings for me, David. Deny it if it soothes your conscience, but they are there."

David finally blurted out, "Of course they are there. How could they not be? Do you think that I don't notice that you are beautiful? Everywhere we go every eye is on you. Yet that desire is impotent compared to my other feelings. You are like ether. You waltz through life on a cloud while I carry the world on my shoulders. You offer to relieve Atlas of his burden, how could I resist?"

"You seem to be doing quite well."

"You don't believe that."

She paused. "No. I know that you aren't." Her voice rose. "So let someone else carry the world for a while. You cannot change the past or rectify the world's ills. And it will only kill you trying. I am yours, David, and all my world. It is time you are given the love you deserve."

"I have always been given the love I deserve. It is I who have shut out that love and brought such pain to MaryAnne."

"Then release her from it and let her get on with her life. From all that you have told me she is wonderful. I cannot imagine that you would marry less. Free her to find love. And free yourself."

"You use my words against me."

"For you. You are good to everyone but yourself. You have whipped yourself with guilt for so long that you don't know how to behave otherwise. You are not responsible for your daughter's death, and whatever twisted satisfaction you derive from blaming yourself won't make it so. Do you know what I think?"

David made no motion to respond, though he was clearly listening.

"I think that you are trying to run yourself to death. You are more gaunt each time I see you. You look like you haven't slept in a week. Someone has to save you from yourself. And it ought to be me, because I love you."

Her words pierced him as deeply as her gaze.

"I have never loved anyone so madly or desperately before. All the good in you, your loyalty, your kindness. I want you for my own, and I know that you feel the same way."

David sat quietly for a moment. "I need to think this over."

She leaned over the table and kissed him. "I will make you very happy, David. I promise you."

Then she kissed him on the lips, and this time David did not resist. She withdrew, then stood from the table, her gaze still fixed on his. "I'll be waiting for your call."

CHAPTER 19

Whiskey Row

"It is strange to me that two women could share such close proximity in my mind, yet be worlds apart. And only one of them cares to be there."

DAVID PARKIN'S DIARY.
JANUARY 12, 1934

The perpetual noise of the metropolis wove through David's broken sleep, and at four twenty-seven he woke and lay on the rigid bed thinking about MaryAnne and Dierdre. MaryAnne had never before seemed so far away. He had never felt so alone. When the blinds glowed beneath the dawn light, he shaved, dressed, then lay back on the bed, and, without intending to, fell back asleep. When he finally woke, he checked his wristwatch and found it nearly eleven. He splashed water in his face, grabbed his jacket, then hurried down to the lobby. It was a cold day, and the bellboy rubbed his hands together as David approached.

"Taxi, sir?"

David nodded, and the man stepped out into the street and, placing a silver whistle to his lips, hailed the first of the line of cabs that awaited the hotel's patrons. He opened the door for David, who handed him a quarter. The driver looked up into his rearview mirror.

"Where to, fella?"

"Do you know this place?" David handed the driver the paper with the tenement's address. The driver confirmed the destination, then handed it back.

"You sure you want to go there, fella? It's a rough spot of town."

"I am sure."

"All right, then."

He put the motorcar in gear and started off towards the "back of the yards" and the tenements of Whiskey Row. The city's landscape and architecture became increasingly miserable as they approached the blight of the meatpacking district and its surrounding fertilizer mills and dumps, all divulging their presence with their putrid contributions to the local air. Smoke rose from squat stacks atop the myriad buildings, concealed behind high fences where each morning faceless men, women, and children of destitution lined up for daily wages amid the greenbackers and socialists who proselytized in their ranks. Though they came from all lands, they were but one nationality and one tongue—they were the impoverished, and their dialect was the voice of desperation. Even still, they, too, embraced the local mores of selective racism and shunned the Negroes who competed with them for work. Even the unionists, who espoused fiscal equality, shunned the blacks on the grounds that they were used as scabs—strikebreakers—only to be discarded by the plant owners after their objectives were met. There were no politics to the Negroes, only hunger.

Further south, David rolled up the taxi's window as the rank smell had reached intolerable levels and the driver pointed out the fetid waters of Bubbly Creek, where the blood and carcasses of the slaughtered animals were discarded and the stench was born.

At the mouth of the Troop Street bridge, he could see the jagged rooftops of the tenements huddled tightly together, as a mouth of crooked teeth—as crowded in structure as they were in inhabitants of their damp and sullen rooms. The streets outside the tenements were litter strewn and desolate, except for a few vagrants, who walked with vacant eyes and spoke loudly to unseen companions, and the smallest of children of Slav or Lithuanian descent, who played, barefoot, in the unpaved streets of the slums—as they were too young to be of value to the packing houses.

The cab stopped in front of a stone-slab entryway, and David examined the frame house. Its windows—those exposed to the street—were clouded by dirt or replaced with wood panels where glass had broken. A yard toilet was visible at the side of the residence, surrounded by the litter that seemed to accumulate everywhere in the slums and piled up in drifts against the houses' foundations like windswept snow. He confirmed the address, then ascended the tenement's short steps and pounded on the door. About a minute later he heard the approach of hobbling footsteps. The door swung open to a hard and surly woman dressed in soiled clothing that hung from the obese body in crumpled drapes. She was old, and her face appeared even more ancient than her advanced years— pocked and blemished by the sun.

"Whad'ya want?" she asked harshly.

"I am looking for a Mrs. Talbot," David replied.

The woman gazed on, cupping a hand to her ear. "Whad'ya say?"

David raised his voice. "I am looking for Mrs. Talbot."

"Whad'ya want her fer?"

"Do you know her?"

"Whad'ya want her fer?" she repeated.

"I was told that she knew my mother—Rosalyn King."

She stared at him for a moment, then replied in a hoarse, but calmer, voice, "That's a name I never thought I'd hear again."

She glanced suspiciously at the taxi. "Who's that with you?"

"The cab driver."

The woman stared at him dubiously, but decided him harmless.

David gestured towards the lobby. "May I come in?"

"Ya want to come inside?"

"Please."

She stepped away from the door, and David followed her tedious motion as she hobbled up a short flight of stairs to an open room. The building reeked of rotting wood and other stenches from undistinguishable sources. The room was dingy and as battered as its absent boarders. Holes were broken through the lath and plaster walls, and the tobacco-stained floor was littered with whiskey bottles and food cans, infested with cockroaches. A bare mattress lay in one corner of the room next to a small coal stove. Beneath the room's only window, a single water faucet emptied into a stained washbasin. The woman motioned to a dilapidated wooden chair.

"This is where she lived?" David asked in repulsion.

"More'n three years." She sniffed, then wiped her nose with her sleeve. "Rose owed me money, you know."

David continued to survey the room. "I will pay some of her debt."

The woman's face twisted into a ghastly and toothless expression only vaguely definable as a smile.

"How'd you find the place?"

"The owners of the Thalia Theater . . ."

"Screws!" she screamed, her cheeks flushed. "Niggardly, stingy, tightwad, penny-pinchin' screws!"

She was left scowling and breathless by the tirade, and David waited for her to calm.

"You said my mother lived here for three years."

"Least three years."

"Can you tell me what she was like?"

"Rose was just Rose. Hungry for somethin' like it just ate at her. Some folk just ain't ever gonna be content. Grew kinda peculiar in the end. Spoke her name like someone might recognize it. R–ose K–ing," the woman mocked, holding the vowels of both names. "Talked 'bout herself like she was another person. Rose King did this. Rose King don't like that."

"I was told that you might have a letter that she left for me."

"A letter? Who told you that?"

David avoided the trap. "Just heard."

"Don't know about no letter," she said, dismissing the query. She suddenly cackled. "Paranoid too, Rose was. Always was the conspiracies. Blamed her failure on the damned Trust. She never said 'the Trust,' always said, 'damned Trust,' like it was its name." She interrupted herself, "You know, I think I might got something of hers." She stood up and walked over to a closet. As she searched through its rubble, David examined an ancient playbill still tacked to the wall.

"Is this my mother?"

The woman laughed and turned from her search. "What are ya, a rube? That's famous ol' Minnie Fisk, the actress. Your mother idolized Minnie. Had her playbills all stuck up to the walls, while she labored as a scrubwoman. She used to say that Minnie Fisk was made famous for the part of a scrubwoman, and she did a more convincing job of it every day. Cleaned a good toilet, Rose. Like to see someone get Minnie Fisk to do that."

David sat back down.

"She was tough as shoe leather. Hard to believe

she did herself in. Just before, she kept saying that she oughta pack up and go to California. They make movies in California. It's easy work, the movies. But she never went." She said as if it had just occurred to her, "Maybe she should've went."

"You were looking for something," David reminded her.

"Oh, yeah, that box. Rose left a box of her stuff." She buried her head back into the closet. "Tripped over that thing for years. Damned if I don't know where it is now." After another minute she concluded her search. "Guess I musta just thrown it out."

David frowned in disappointment. "You're sure it's not somewhere else?"

"Ain't no place else." She pointed to the closet. "You're welcome to look yourself."

David stood, no longer able to bear the woman's or the room's repulsiveness.

"How much did my mother owe you?"

"Well, it been a long time. She didn't pay for nearly six months. Maybe twenty dollars."

David handed her thirty in three bills. "There's interest included with that."

Her eyes lit at the sight of money. "That's jake I never thought I'd see." She snatched the money, afraid that he might change his mind.

David reached into his pocket. "Here's my calling card. If you do find something, I am staying at the Drake Hotel."

As he walked from the building, she dropped the card to the floor with the other refuse.

David climbed back into the car.

"Back to the Drake," he said.

The driver happily obliged.

✦

As they crossed a steel-girdered bridge just a few blocks from the tenement, David asked, "What bridge is this?"

"The Troop Street."

"Hold up a moment," he said. "Just pull up to the side of the road past the bridge."

"Your dime. Meter's still running."

David climbed out of the car. Near the entrance to the bridge a ragged peddler, buffeted by the cold winds, stood next to a flower cart filled with a hodgepodge of jugs and kettles, make-do receptacles for his cut flowers—a potpourri of tulips, snapdragons and mums, and heather, gerber daisies, and roses.

David approached the peddler.

"I would like a rose. A red one."

The man spoke with a heavy, Lithuanian accent. "Don't sell 'em as one. Sell a bunch. Two bits a bunch."

David handed the man a coin, which the decrepit man exchanged for a bouquet, then drew out one stem, and let the rest fall to the ground. He advanced along the pedestrian walkway onto the bridge.

A quarter way up the expanse, he stopped and

climbed atop an iron girder of the bridge's trestle-work, then, clinging to a weathered cable, stared out over the water. His mother's last sight. More than sixty feet below, the azure, windswept river churned into meringue crests, sometimes obscured beneath a frozen mist. The banks of the river were steep and sharply cut. If one survived a fall from the bridge, they would be paralyzed by hypothermia and unable to climb the steep embankment—even if they had the Herculean strength required to cross the river's icy torrent. He stood only five inches from his own death, and the simplicity of that fact was not lost on him. Where was his MaryAnne? Not what continent, or even where her heart laid, but, rather, where was she in his own heart? He remembered a day when he had knelt before her and, on bended knee, held her shaking hand and proposed their marriage. Her eyes were wet, tears born anew in celebration of his love instead of the agony she felt just moments before as she spoke of her wretched circumstance and her shameful pregnancy. His love had rescued her, she had said, and now he wondered if it would rescue him. He gazed out over the deadly waters for many minutes. Then, an astonishing thought came to him—an insight that had eluded him since his daughter's death. In view of the murky waters he began to see things very clearly.

He released the rose and watched it fall, dancing on the strings of the wind's caprices until it disappeared from sight into the turbid water. He tarried in the spot for a few more minutes, then, with purpose, stepped down from the ledge and walked back to the idling cab. At his return, the driver looked relieved.

He said after David had climbed back in, "Thought for a moment you might be thinkin' of jumpin'."

"You didn't lose your fare," David answered. "Take me back to the Drake."

CHAPTER 20

Catherine's
Telegram

"It is of little consolation to learn of my mother's wretched past. For as miserable as it was she still chose it over me."

DAVID PARKIN'S DIARY.
JANUARY 12, 1934

As David reentered the hotel, he was mistaken for a vagrant and accosted by the Drake's security. To his misfortune, he carried nothing to identify himself, except a suspiciously large wad of money and his room key, which, once revealed, produced the unfortunate effect of convincing the guard that the vagabond had fallen on one of the hotel's guests, emptied his purse, and now sought to further capitalize on his felony by cleaning out his room as well. The Chicago police were summoned, and such commotion ensued that it was noticed by one of the hotel's bellboys—a recipient of David's generosity—who rushed to David's defense and identification. A mortified and contrite guard followed David into the hotel and showered him with fervent apologies until David assured the man that he would not complain to the hotel management of the incident if he would just leave him alone. As David crossed the crowded lobby, he was flagged by the concierge.

"How are you today, Mr. Parkin?"

"I am fine," David replied tersely, still agitated from his brief detention.

He held out an envelope. "You have just received an urgent telegram."

David took the note.

MR. DAVID PARKIN. DRAKE HOTEL. CHICAGO, ILLINOIS.

LAWRENCE SUFFERED STROKE. TAKEN TO HOUSE. RETURN IMMEDIATELY. CATHERINE.

David turned to the concierge. "Do you have a train schedule?"

"Yes, sir," he replied, reaching for the timetable.

"When does the next train depart for Salt Lake?"

He ran his finger down the page. "Ten minutes past five. A little over two hours from now."

"Thank you." David handed him a five-dollar bill. "Thank you for all of your assistance."

"It has been my pleasure, Mr. Parkin. Would you like me to call the train depot."

"Please. If you would."

As he turned to go, the concierge stopped him again. "Mr. Parkin. Pardon my oversight. This parcel arrived for you as well."

He set a large beige envelope, stamped with a Chicago address, on the edge of the counter. It was from the Thalia Theater. David tore back its flap as he walked to the elevator. Inside was a letter written on embossed stationery, a playbill, a pair of silver-rimmed eyeglasses, and a skeleton key tied with a saffron ribbon.

✦

Mr. Parkin,
Your visit of yesterday was so unanticipated, we
fear we behaved rather crassly. Please accept
our sincerest apologies. We neglected to present
to you these articles that once belonged to your
mother. Also, Mr. Sinclair came across this
playbill and thought it might be of interest.
Please receive them with our kindest regards.
At your service,

THEODORE CUTHBERT AND ALMA F. SINCLAIR

❖

David guessed the key belonged to the tenement
house, examined the glasses, then extracted the
playbill. Its cover was graced by the rotund and bux-
om form of a woman. A wide-brimmed hat partially
shadowed her face yet failed to conceal the beauty of
her haunting eyes. He looked at it briefly, then returned it to the envelope and went to his room to pack.

❖

"It has been a mistake living my life in the
past. One cannot ride a horse backwards and
still hold its reins."

DAVID PARKIN'S DIARY. JANUARY 13, 1934

❖

David lay on the sleeping berth of the westbound train—his mind filled with emotions as converse as the direction itself. The playbill's picture of his mother haunted him, and when he slept he slept fitfully, revealed in the dark shadows of his eyes.

In his sudden departure he had left unfinished business, for he had not had the opportunity to speak with Dierdre, and his thoughts now revolved in a kaleidoscope of four women: MaryAnne, Andrea, Dierdre, and Rose—a very different image than the one he had carried with him to Chicago. On the bridge's expanse he had experienced a quiet epiphany, and though the identity of the author who had left the letter at the angel was now a greater mystery than ever, it was no longer of any import. Whether he had received Catherine's telegram or not, he was ready to go home.

The lumbering train entered the Salt Lake depot late Thursday afternoon beneath affable, cloud-pocked skies. He reclaimed his automobile from a dirt lot south of the station and drove home. At the opening of the front door, Catherine rushed down the stairs to greet him.

"Welcome home, David!"

She threw her arms around him. He had lost weight and his complexion was wan, his eyes revealing the succession of sleepless nights. She scolded him.

"You have not taken care of yourself."

"No worse than usual. How is Lawrence faring?"

"He is doing a little better. I have put him up in the east guest room."

"Good. We have much to talk about."

Catherine looked distressed by the remark.

"David, that won't be possible."

He looked at her quizzically.

"The stroke left him unable to speak. He is responding now, a little, but I do not know if he recalls anything from before. I am not even certain that he knows who I am."

David's face fell, and he grasped the stairs' banister.

"Oh, my friend," he said. He started up the stairway, followed by Catherine. As he entered the dimly lit room he could see Lawrence's husky form shrouded by thick quilts. He walked to his side.

"Lawrence?"

At first there was no motion, then Lawrence slowly turned towards him, mumbling incoherently. David took his hand. "How are you, my friend?"

Lawrence said nothing. David's eyes moistened.

"How long has he been like this?"

"I found him unconscious Monday morning last. He is doing a little better since then, but the doctor does not anticipate any more improvement."

David took her arm and led her out of Lawrence's hearing.

"What else has the doctor said?"

"There is grave danger of another stroke or heart attack." Catherine could see in David's eyes the sadness her news produced. She embraced him again. "You must be exhausted. Let me get you some supper."

David looked back at his silent friend. "Thank you for all that you have done, Catherine. I will sit with him awhile."

"If I had known you would be returning today, I would have prepared a more fitting meal. I have only made bread and soup."

"After the train's cuisine, that is feast enough."

She left the room as David returned to the quiet bedside. David sat still for a moment, then suddenly began to speak with Lawrence as it had been before—as if they sat around the warped table of Lawrence's shanty and Lawrence's deep eyes reflected the glow of his pipe while words of deep consideration filled the air.

"I just arrived back from Chicago . . . I don't know if you remember . . . I was going to go look for my mother . . . because I found that letter and thought she was still alive." David pulled a slipped corner of a blanket up over Lawrence's muscular shoulder. "It didn't go quite how I expected it would, but I got my answers. Turns out that my mother never amounted to anything, and she ended up jumping from a bridge. My whole life I have felt like I needed to talk to her, to ask her why she left me. But I realized that what I really wanted to know is why I wasn't worthy of her love. That is something she couldn't have answered, because I was worthy of her love, whether she gave it to me or not. Every child is worthy of love." David sniffed, then rubbed his nose. "In a way, she was also looking for love. She thought she could find it in the applause of an audience. But what good is the love of strangers if your life is of no value to your own child?"

David paused.

"I met this other woman. Her name is Dierdre. You would like her—she's a firebrand. How would you say it . . ." He smiled. ". . . hotter than July jam. Anyway, something stuck her good. I don't know what she saw in me, she could do much better. The man part of me didn't have any objections, just the husband part. I have to admit that it felt good to be cared for by her. Made me feel young again. But she wasn't MaryAnne. You were right about that tree thing, the love tree, or whatever you called it. I am not ready to let the tree die. MaryAnne and I have given each other the best of ourselves and maybe the worst, too, but either way, we both own a significant portion of each other. That's not something you can just walk away from. When you are feeling better I am going to go to England to bring her back. What do you think of that?"

Lawrence did not make a sound, and David sighed.

"Where have you gone to, my friend?" He sat back in the darkness and, once again, was joined by the too familiar companionship of loss.

✦

"It is an awkward thing for a loved one to retain their breath but lose their faculties. I feel as though my heart has been cheated, as I have lost a friend and am not allowed to grieve his passing."

DAVID PARKIN'S DIARY. JANUARY 16, 1934

Later that same evening, as the city was cloaked beneath a blackened curtain pierced by the pinpricks of a million stars, a tall, dark-haired woman stepped from a taxi that had parked out front of the Parkin mansion. She carried only a bag, its strap parting her breast over a grey wool coat. She ascended the home's driveway and pounded the great brass knocker on the front door. Catherine met the stranger, then, after a brief exchange, invited her in. A few moments later Catherine entered Lawrence's infirmary. With animated motion she gestured to David, and he came to the doorway.

"There is a woman in the foyer that has come to see Lawrence," Catherine whispered.

"Who is she?"

"Her name is Sophia. Do you know her?"

David remembered the name from an earlier conversation.

"No. But Lawrence has spoken of her. Who does she say she is?"

Catherine's eyes widened. "She says she is Lawrence's daughter."

CHAPTER 21

Sophia

"Sophia's arrival at this time is too fantastic for mere coincidence . . . the fact that Lawrence had a daughter explains many things, but most of all why he held our daughter Andrea so dear."

DAVID PARKIN'S DIARY.
JANUARY 15, 1934

David stood on the parapet overlooking the foyer. Down below, a woman, slightly older than himself, sat on a walnut side chair, quietly looking down at the marble floor. He descended the stairway, and when she saw him, she rose, apprehensively following his descent with her eyes. Her skin was a fair mahogany, and though her features were dark, they were also sharp and hinted of European descent, giving her a Mediterranean appearance. Still, in her deep-set, umber eyes and the gentle slope of her jaw, he could see her father's endowments.

"Mr. Parkin, I am Sophia Disera," she said in beautiful diction.

David extended his hand. "Please call me David."

"Thank you. I was told that my father is being cared for here. I have come a long way to see him."

David extended his hand. "Allow me to take your coat."

She slipped the garment off, and he hung it on the room's walnut hall tree.

"How did you know that your father was here?"

"I didn't. I came to inquire if you knew of his whereabouts. A man with a fruit cart over on Brigham Street said that you and my father were friends. Your housekeeper told me that he is here."

"Are you aware of his condition?"

Her countenance turned more anxious. "His condition? Your housekeeper said that you have been
caring for him. Is he ill?"

"Lawrence has had a stroke. He can no longer
speak. We have no way of knowing if he even rec-
ognizes our voices."

"Your voices?"

"Your father is blind."

In shock, she lifted a hand to her breast. "Then I
am too late," she said, sitting back down and clasp-
ing her hands in her lap. After a moment she said,
"I should still like to see him."

"Of course." David held out his hand and helped
her rise. "He is upstairs." David led her to the corridor outside the guest room and opened its door,
revealing Lawrence's silhouette. She walked in
alone, shutting the door behind herself. David sat
down outside the door. From time to time he could
hear her gentle voice, but always to no response.
Fifteen minutes later she came from the room. She
sobbed heavily. As he approached her, she collapsed. David called for Catherine, who rushed upstairs from the kitchen. She opened the door of the
adjoining guest room for David, who carried in the
woman and laid her on the bed. Catherine returned
with a damp cloth which she laid across the
woman's forehead. Only a few minutes later
Sophia's eyes fluttered, then opened. A confused
expression blanketed her face.

"You have fainted, Sophia," David said softly.

She closed her eyes. "It was such a shock."

She looked again at the two strangers who stood over her. "I am sorry to cause such trouble. I should return to my hotel."

"Nonsense," Catherine said. "You will stay here tonight."

"You will remain with us," David concurred. "Just rest."

A few moments after Catherine had left to care for Lawrence, Sophia said to David, "I only learned that my father was alive two months ago. When my mother died. The last words on her lips were for Lawrence."

"What is your mother's name?"

"Margaret."

He nodded. "Of course. That is why he was behaving so strangely. He must have known of her death. How did you learn of him?"

"After my mother died I began to go through her things. I came across a large trunk filled with correspondence. There were more than a thousand letters, dated as far back as 1874. All of them were from Lawrence. I spent the next three weeks piecing together their story through their letters. My father met my mother when he was a soldier in the tenth cavalry my grandfather commanded. Over several years they fell in love and were married. Not legally, of course. It was unthinkable for a white woman to marry a Negro—even if no one else wanted her. So they decided that they would perform their own ceremony.

"They took their own vows and hid their love behind secret rendezvous. Every few weeks my mother would supposedly go off to visit a college friend, and he would take leave. In public he traveled as her valet, and no one ever suspected. The arrangement worked fine until she got pregnant. As she started to show, they got scared. My mother knew her father would have Lawrence lynched if he found out. So they fabricated an alibi that she had eloped with a Cuban soldier. They had a falsified wedding document. She even pretended to receive letters from him for a while. Then one day she informed her parents that her husband had been killed in combat. It was a lie I lived with my whole life.

"Despite their love they took a vow that they would never see each other again." Her eyes filled with tears. "I used to try to imagine what my father looked like. In my imagination he was always a tall, beautiful Spaniard, with flowing hair and the statuesque physique of a warrior."

"Your father was a great man, Sophia."

Sophia looked down. "I want to believe that."

"What did you mean by 'no one else wanted your mother'?"

"No one, except Lawrence, ever called my mother beautiful. My mother was a beautiful woman, David, but not because society would bestow the title. She was beautiful because her spirit was beautiful. The world shunned her as disfigured and hideous. Most of my mother's face was covered with a cruel birthmark. I don't think Lawrence could see the blemish. In a way he was the same as her, they were both victims of their skin."

"What a shock this must all be to you."

"My mother didn't want anyone to know that I was half Negro—she even hid it from me. She prayed that I would be fair-skinned. A 'pe-ola.' She straightened my hair with pomade and a curling iron." She smiled sadly. "Imagine my surprise when I found out that my father was a Negro—that I am a Negro. Every belief that I accepted from society I now have to atone for with my own self-perspective. I do not feel any different than I did yesterday. I do not look or speak or think differently. But today I am a Negro. Am I to think less of myself?

"Mama worked hard to teach me that people are people and not to be judged by their appearances. I once thought that she taught me this because of her own flesh, her own mark. It wasn't so. It was to save me. She taught me so that I would not hate myself someday."

"Your mother was wise."

Sophia reflected on her mother and smiled distantly. "She was a good woman. She always knew the right thing to say."

"That is what I always said of MaryAnne."

"MaryAnne is your housekeeper?"

"No. That is Catherine. MaryAnne is my wife."

"She is out tonight?"

David hesitated. "No. She is away."

Sophia sensed that there was more to his answer

and did not pursue it further. After a moment she said, "You know he mentioned you in his letters. He wrote of you as if you walked on water."

"He lied. I have trouble swimming."

She smiled. "In one of the letters he wrote about you claiming to have shot a man that he killed in self-defense. And he told her about your daughter. I feel like I know you, David."

David took her hand. "I am truly sorry that you cannot speak with your father. For both of you." He glanced over at the mantelpiece clock. "You better get some rest. I have to go into work early, but I will be back in the afternoon. What hotel holds your things?"

"The Beehive Room."

"If you do not object, I will pick up your things for you on my way back from work. Until then I am sure that we have whatever you may need at the house. Catherine will see to you."

She smiled gratefully. "Thank you, David. For everything."

CHAPTER 22

Boggs's
Dismissal

"The winds of depression have blown the dust from the horsewhip, noose, and hood . . ."

A NEWSPAPER CLIPPING
FOUND IN DAVID PARKIN'S
DIARY, BELIEVED GIVEN
TO HIM BY GIBBS

David departed early for work in anticipation of the mountain of documents that was certain to have piled up in his absence. As the red-bricked edifice of the Parkin Machinery Company came to view on the corner of second south, he noticed a crowd of considerable size gathered at the west end of his building. It was not unusual for a crowd of indigents to be gathered near his business to inquire for daily work, only this morning their ranks had swelled, joined by men and women dressed in business attire, drawn as spectators to the same site by some mutual force of fascination.

David could not see what held such interest until he parked his car and stepped to the curb. Hanging from his building's awning, from a rope around his neck, was a black man's lifeless body. David knew the man as Carville, an employee of nearly twenty years. He was a good man with a cheerful disposition. He had well earned his position as the company's night foreman, and only three years previous David had recommended the promotion himself. David angrily shoved his way to the front of the throng, removed his coat, and began swinging it angrily at the crowd.

"Get out of here, you vultures! Get away from my building!"

Slowly, the crowd began to dissipate. Taking a pocket knife from his trousers, he cut the rope and, despite his effort, the body fell heavily to the concrete sidewalk. The man's hands had been tied behind his back, then lashed again to his feet. David covered the body with his jacket, then recognizing one of the spectators as an employee, ordered the man to assist him in carrying the body inside before the other employees arrived.

✦

Gibbs entered David's office with a grave disposition. He could not read David's face.

"Is it true?"

"Would that it wasn't," he replied, his voice laced with disgust. "I don't even know if he had children."

"He did," Gibbs said. "His wife brought dinner down at night. Sometimes she'd have a little one hanging from her leg."

"You tell his wife to keep coming to collect his payroll," David said. He shook his head. "Why didn't you tell me about the fire in the yard?"

"I intended to. I just thought it would be best to wait until you returned. I couldn't see the point in telling you while you were still in Chicago."

David replied nothing.

"I am sorry. I thought I was doing the right thing."

"You did, Gibbs. There was nothing I could have

done but given in. And that wasn't an option."
David leaned back in his chair, held back by the
one foot resting on the edge of the desk. "This was
done by my employees. How else would they have
known Carville's hours or his position? Wasn't that
the point? If I won't fire the Negroes, they will
frighten them into leaving."

"You don't know that."

"I am not sure that I don't." He lowered the front
legs of his chair back to the floor. "Get me Judd
Boggs. I want to see what he knows of the affair."

"You think he will tell you?"

"In not so many words."

David was more correct than he could have
hoped for. When Boggs arrived at his office, he was
clearly agitated, his movements tight and quick, as
if at any moment he might bolt from the room.
Gibbs stood near the doorway behind Boggs,
which seemed to add to the man's anxiety, as every
few minutes he would glance back around. Before
David could question him about the lynching,
Boggs blurted out in a tremorous voice, "You ain't
thinkin' that I done hung the nigger?"

David glanced over to Gibbs. "I couldn't imagine
such a thing."

"I didn't hang him. Didn't even tie his hands."

David looked sharply at Boggs.

"Did you see Carville this morning?"

"I ain't seen nothin'. Not a thing."

"I never mentioned that his hands were tied. How
did you know that?"

Panic flashed across Boggs's face. "Buck nigger like that, you'd hafta tie 'em back."

"You seem to know a good deal about lynching."

Boggs turned paler. "I'd like to go now, Mr. Parkin."

David stared at him, his emotion raging beneath a dispassionate veneer. "You can go. Your services are no longer required at my company."

The words fell like a death sentence, and, during the Depression, often held the same weight.

"I am fired?"

"Despite Carville's unfortunate departure, we still have too many employees. I was sure that you would have no objection because you are concerned with my best interest. Aren't you, Mr. Boggs?"

The man turned from white to crimson, yet remained frozen beneath David's cool gaze.

"Payday was Saturday, you have two days' wages coming. Pay him up, Gibbs, and get him out of my building."

Gibbs approached the shaken man and escorted him out of the office.

CHAPTER 23

A Surprise
Return

". . . I would have sooner expected Hoover's re-election than what awaited me tonight."

DAVID PARKIN'S DIARY.
JANUARY 16, 1934

It was twilight when David returned home, and the mountains were cast in the salmon hue of the sun's departure. On his entrance, he was passed by a wide-fendered taxi leaving his driveway, occupied only by the driver. He parked his car and entered the side door through the kitchen. As he walked into the foyer, he beheld a leather trunk at the foot of the stairway. And then MaryAnne.

She gazed at him apprehensively, and he looked back at her in quiet surprise—as if he had encountered an apparition, and, in truth, he considered a specter's appearance more likely.

MaryAnne spoke first. "Hello, David."

David just stared, unsure of his own feelings and less of hers. He wanted to run to her, to embrace her, but there was no assurance that she would not turn from him or even that she had come to stay. MaryAnne turned away from his gaze.

"Catherine wired me about Lawrence . . ." she said.

His heart fell.

"I am glad that you could come back for him."

"If it is permissible, I would like to stay in the east guest room."

"No. You take our . . ." He corrected himself, ". . . the bedroom."

"Thank you."

"Someone is already staying in the east guest room."

She looked at him quizzically.

". . . Sophia."

MaryAnne was surprised and upset by David's answer.

"Who is Sophia?"

"She is Lawrence's daughter."

MaryAnne lifted a hand to her breast. "Oh, my . . . a daughter?"

Catherine suddenly appeared at the crest of the stairway, was momentarily baffled by what she saw, then squealed when she realized the woman at the foot of the stairs was MaryAnne.

"MaryAnne. You have returned."

"Just for a while," David said curtly.

MaryAnne glanced towards him and frowned. Catherine descended the stairway to embrace MaryAnne.

"It is so good to see you again."

"I came as soon as I received your letter about Lawrence."

Catherine glaced anxiously at David, then lifted the bag at MaryAnne's feet. "Let's get you settled."

Without a word, David watched them ascend the stairway, then went to his den.

Upstairs, in the master bedchamber, Catherine began to unpack MaryAnne's trunk into the drawers of the armoire, while MaryAnne, at Catherine's insistence, sat idle on the bed, tempted to ask a thousand questions.

"How is Lawrence?"

"I am afraid that he is not doing well."

MaryAnne sighed. "Is it true that he has a daughter?"

"Apparently. She arrived late last night. Not even David knew of her."

As Catherine continued her dispersal of the trunk's articles she grew more quiet, and MaryAnne could not bear the mounting tension. "Catherine, please don't be angry with me."

She looked up. "I'm sorry, MaryAnne. I don't mean to be angry. I just feel so betrayed. I have gone over in my mind what you said the morning before you left, relived every word you said, and it drives me mad knowing that you knew and you didn't tell me. I guess it was presumptuous to believe myself your best friend."

"You are, Catherine. I just couldn't bear to tell David, and it wouldn't be right to tell you and not him." She looked towards the open door. "He is being so cold. He hates me now."

"I have never seen him in such pain—even when Andrea died. You broke his heart, Mary. But you misunderstand him. He fears you, but he doesn't hate you."

"Fears me? Why?"

"Who else can inflict on him such pain?"

MaryAnne bowed her head into her open palms.

"This was a mistake. I never should have come back."

At this, Catherine came over and sat on the bed next to MaryAnne, taking MaryAnne's hands in hers. "I'm sorry. You had to expect it would be difficult. But it wasn't a mistake. I am so happy to see you again. Even if it is for a brief time."

"Bless you, Catherine," MaryAnne said, and the two women fell into each other's embrace.

✦

"I came home to find that MaryAnne had returned. She promptly made it clear that she does not intend to stay. My heart, of necessity, has become acrobatic."

DAVID PARKIN'S DIARY. JANUARY 16, 1934

✦

Sophia spent the better part of the next week sitting at Lawrence's side, sometimes talking, sometimes just staring with wet eyes, and never ceasing to hope for some sign—some acknowledgment that he understood who she was.

She had not planned to stay in Salt Lake City for this length of time, and she knew that her husband and family would soon require her return. As Lawrence's condition neither improved nor declined, she decided that it was nearing the time that she would return home. Friday night, the eve before her scheduled departure, she did not leave his side. Around midnight she slid her hand into his.

"I don't know what you understand. But I must say this, as much for me as you. I want you to know that Mother loved you with all of her heart. It was your name on her lips when she died."

Lawrence's eyes showed no sign of comprehension, but his breath seemed more shallow and halting.

"She never told me about you. I learned of you through the letters you wrote to her." She paused, and her voice was suddenly charged by emotion. "Why did you never come to me? Were you so afraid of being discovered that you wouldn't come to your own daughter?" She began to tear up and laid her head against his chest. "I am sorry. I am only thinking of myself. This is so unfair. Lord, let him know it's me. Please remove the clouds from his mind."

Lawrence's dark, brooding eyes looked steadily ahead.

She took a deep breath, forcing herself to regain her composure. "You have three grandchildren, one boy and two girls. You would be proud of them, they are all good children. The youngest is a little mischievous. He is now sixteen years of age. He was named after you. I didn't know it, but he was. Mother was adamant we name him Lawrence. We call him little Larry most of the time." She caressed the rough hand again, then, overwhelmed by sadness, again lowered her head and said softly, "Father."

Suddenly, the hand squeezed tightly around hers. She looked up into his granite face and could see where a single tear had fallen down his cheek.

"You know."

She leaned close to him as tears began to streak down her own cheeks. "You know."

The great hand rose to the back of her head, pulling her closer, and Sophia wept into her father's chest.

✦

Sophia was at Lawrence's side when he died Sunday afternoon. His passing was not a peaceful one. A massive heart attack clutched Lawrence, and Sophia cried out for David. By the time David arrived, Lawrence lay gasping his last breaths.

Sophia trembled, her hands raised to her cheeks. "I don't know what has happened."

Catherine and MaryAnne both entered the room, and Catherine had called for the doctor. David propped a pillow under Lawrence's head and held the big man from the bed's edge. When the doctor arrived, he parted Lawrence's flannel top and placed the steel orb of his stethoscope on his chest.

"He has had a heart attack."

Sophia cupped her mouth with her hands.

"What can be done?" David asked.

"Nothing to save him. I can give ether for the pain."

"Do it," David said. When the doctor had administered the vial's dosage, David herded everyone but Sophia from the room. Sophia held her father's hand as he lay dying. When he took his final breath, she bowed her head over him and said, "I love you, Papa."

CHAPTER 24

The Funeral

"When we bury someone we love, we must also bury a part of our heart. But we should not bemoan this loss. Our hearts, perhaps, are all they can take with them."

DAVID PARKIN'S DIARY.
JANUARY 28, 1934

"Your father wanted to be buried next to your mother," David said.

"It would be the right thing—but it isn't possible," Sophia said. "Mother was entombed in the family sepulchre. The family would never allow it."

"Then, with your blessing, we will have him buried in our family's plot, near his stone angel."

She looked at him gratefully. "I am sure he would have wanted it that way."

"I will see to it."

✦

The sexton of the Salt Lake City cemetery was an olive-skinned man of Italian descent, succinct of stature—a head shorter than most of his gender—with silver, wiry hair that grew vertical as if in compensation for the height nature had slighted him. He had come to work at the cemetery as a youth when his father, a driller at the Oquirrh copper mines, had been killed in the pit and the cemetery's previous sexton felt pity on the poor family and offered him, the oldest male of the clan, an apprenticeship. He had been there since.

The sexton's home was a weathered cottage of

ginger-tinted stucco mostly concealed by the vines
and ivy that climbed its walls and chimney and
smothered its paned windows.

The sexton pulled his suspenders up over his
shoulders and greeted David at the door.

"Mr. Parkin, isn't it?"

"Yes. I need to arrange for a burial."

The man's thick eyebrows knitted in consolation.
He had long before mastered the art of mixing
business with condolence.

"You considering any particular part of the cemetery?"

"Up near our daughter."

The man nodded knowingly. "The angel monument." He grasped the curved handle of a black
cane and then his jacket. "Nice part of the yard.
Let's go on up and take a look. My cart is near."

The old man's cart, drawn by a single, aged
palomino, pulled them slowly to the center of the
cemetery. The snow on the knoll was crystallized
beneath the winter sun and pristine, as it had not
been visited since MaryAnne's departure. As the
seraph came into view, David's chest grew heavy.
Unlike his wife, David did not often visit the angel,
as it did not bring him condolence. The sexton
pulled back on the reins lightly and, requiring little
persuasion, the horse stopped, lowering its head to
feed on the scant greenery that poked through the
crusted snow. They both climbed down from the
buckboard.

"Them your plots right there," the sexton said.

He walked them off, delineating their circumfer-
ence in the snow with his cane. He paused at the
upper slope of the knoll. "How about this one? Just
a little north of yours."

David glanced around the yard. A northern
breeze whistled through the webbed canopy of
the naked trees overhead. It was the season of
the place. His gaze settled back on the plot. "It
will do. What is the tallest monument in your
cemetery?"

The sexton cast his eyes southward. "Over there.
The Mormon prophet's."

From their vantage point they could see the pin-
nacle of the granite spire above the rest.

"It should be one inch taller than that."

The sexton was astonished. "Gonna cost a small
fortune. Must've been one important gentleman."

David nodded.

"Politician or businessman?"

"He was a war hero."

The man squinted. "Didn't read about no hero's
death. Usually there'll be something in the *Tribune*
or *Deseret News*."

"There was no mention of his death. He is a Negro."

The sexton's face turned ashen at the revelation.
"Mr. Parkin, you can't go buryin' a Negro up in this
part of the cemetery."

"Why not?"

"It's against the law burying a Negro with white
folk. Coloreds have their own place."

"Where?"

"In the colored section. On the south side."

David knew the place, a crowded, overgrown weed patch contained by a black spear fence.

"This is the city cemetery. He should be buried here."

The sexton's face twisted. "There'll be complaints."

David glanced around the graveyard. "You get complaints from them in here?"

"Well, no, but . . ." he stammered, "the folks that come."

"It's not their home."

"Maybe not, but it's against the law."

David pondered the dilemma. "Where does the law actually take offense in burying a Negro near a white man?"

"Don't follow ya."

"What part of the Negro is offensive?"

"What part?"

"It couldn't be the hair, my hair is as dark. In fact, my hair is darker than Lawrence's since he greyed. Couldn't be his eyes. Is it just the skin? Having black flesh?"

"Stands to reason. That's what makes a Negro, ain't it?"

"Is it?"

The old man didn't answer.

"Tell me, how long before the skin starts to decay?"

The macabre question surprised the man. "How

long? Get 'm in the ground, suppose five weeks.
Let 'm sit around in the sun a few days and might
only be three."

"Then these folks buried here aren't really
white."

"Well, most of 'em . . ."

"I don't see where we have a problem here."
David counted out bills from a stack of currency
and handed it to the man. "See to my request."

The man eyed the bills lustfully, then took them.
Still shaking his head, he climbed back into the
carriage. "You a' comin'?"

"No. I'll walk home from here. The body has
been embalmed, I will expect you to come for it tomorrow. We will plan the funeral for the twenty-
eighth."

"Frankly, I don't know why you'd want to go to
such trouble for a Negro buryin'. It's not like black
folk got a soul."

David glared back at the man incredulously, but
was more filled with sadness than anger.

"It is not their souls I worry about."

The sexton pulled the horse's head back, and the
horse plodded forward. When David was alone, he
slowly approached the stone monument. He
glanced at its inscription. Our Little Angel. He
knelt down on one knee before it. In a serene voice
he said, "I've got to tell you something, honey. I am
letting you go. I once thought that to release the
pain was a type of betrayal. I now know that the opposite is true—that the greatest gift I can give to

you is to free you from the burden of my grief. If life is so precious that I mourned the loss of yours, how wrong to throw away mine. I wonder if the loss of my life has caused you the same pain that the loss of yours caused me." He stopped, glanced up to the angel, then dropped his head again. "I know how much you loved your mother. I promise you that I will not close my heart to her again." He looked around the cemetery, and the glare of the yard forced him to squint. "That's all I wanted to say." He closed his eyes for a moment, then rose and walked home.

✦

Only nine were in attendance at Lawrence's interment, including the white, southern, Baptist minister who would perform the rites. At the sexton's insistence, a black minister was not allowed, as the risk of discovery and subsequent controversy was far too great. The sexton's foreboding was not in vain. Two of Lawrence's mourners, fellow soldiers of the Negro 24th cavalry, had arrived early for the funeral and had been noticed by a group that congregated over another service. One of that party confronted the sexton about the Negroes' presence and was told they were grave diggers. The news appeased the inquirer, who expected little more of the race, and would somehow sleep better knowing that the Negroes still knew their place.

The preacher stood at the head of the casket and

MaryAnne, flanked by Catherine and Gibbs, stood to one side, opposite of David, Sophia, and the two soldiers. At the conclusion of the preacher's blessing, David stepped forward.

"I am honored to say a few words about my friend, though I fear I will not do him justice. I don't know that anyone could. Lawrence Flake was a good man. He gave more than he had and expected less than he deserved. In so doing, he left this world a better place. I feel honored that he called me his friend and fortunate to call him mine."

David began to tear up as he looked over to the angel statue that viewed the proceedings with its usual stoicism.

"His giving of his angel statue to our little girl was one of the noblest gestures I have ever beheld. He had hoped that it might someday mark his grave and passersby would know that here lay someone worthy of such a monument. Worthy of common respect. As I said, Lawrence expected less than he deserved. The Bible says that no greater love is there than to lay down your life for another. But I think that would not be difficult for Lawrence, as his life was bitter and not to be envied by any. What he did with his angel was to lay down his hope for the hereafter. I have only seen greatness a few times in my life. I saw it in Lawrence." He raised his head. "That's all I have to say."

MaryAnne looked up at David lovingly, but he turned from her soft eyes. Wiping back her tears, she stepped forward and laid a flower atop the casket. Sophia took David's hand and he put his arm around her. She leaned into him.

"Your words were beautiful. Thank you."

"It was my honor."

When Sophia was ready to leave, the remaining mourners walked back to the automobiles parked to the shoulder of the dirt road. Catherine, MaryAnne, and Elaine had all ridden with Gibbs, as Sophia's luggage filled the backseat of David's automobile, she had planned to catch the train back to Birmingham that very afternoon. David glanced over as Gibbs offered the door to MaryAnne and she thanked him and climbed inside. As Gibbs's car pulled away, MaryAnne glanced back to David, and for a brief moment their eyes met. David turned over the Packard's motor and drove off from the gravesite in a different direction.

C H A P T E R 2 5

The Second
Departure

"I have heard it preached that on Judgment Day our sins will be shouted from the rooftops. I have come to believe that if this is so, it will not be by some heavenly tribunal or something loathsome that crawls beneath, but from our own countenance screaming out to the world who we really are—when the kind and the good, no matter how plain in this life, will shine forth like suns, while the loathsome and dark will cower from their light." "If Heaven is a place where there are no secrets, it would, for some, also be Hell."

DAVID PARKIN'S DIARY.
JANUARY 29, 1934

"I don't mourn for my father," Sophia said as they left the cemetery. She wiped her eyes with a moist handkerchief. "I believe that my parents are finally together in a place where love knows no color . . . nor deformity. But there are things I regret not being able to ask him. I understand the danger that his relationship with my mother posed. But his abandonment was so complete. I will always wonder why he never came to me."

"I can't understand it," David replied. "He was so close to our little girl. I am still astonished that after all these years he never told me he had a daughter."

"I know this will sound terrible, but I have wondered if his fear of being discovered was just greater than his love for me."

David turned from the road, glancing sternly into Sophia's eyes. "Lawrence was no coward. It's just not so."

"I would almost rather hear that he was. Then, at least, I would know why. The unknowing is worse than any truth."

David's countenance relaxed. "You and I have much in common, Sophia. In a sense, your journey is the same as mine. My own mother abandoned me when I was a child. I also went out to find my mother in search of answers. But she had already died."

"What did you hope to find?"

"Understanding of why I was not worthy of her."

"Then your journey was also a failure."

"Not at all. I brought back what I needed."

"What did you learn?"

"To leave the past behind. The answers are not in the past. Healing comes from purpose and purpose resides in our hope of the future." David suddenly pounded the steering wheel with his fist.

"I just remembered a request your father made. He said that if you were to ever come around that he had something for you he kept in a box. I asked him what it was, and he said, 'Your answers.'"

"Where is it?!"

"He kept it under his bed." David glanced at his watch. "Your train doesn't leave for an hour yet. We'll have time if we hurry."

David turned north at Brigham Street and drove to the defunct cannery that supported Lawrence's shanty. The Packard lurched around the side of the building, stopping in front of the black man's former residence. The shanty's door was wide open. They both stepped from the automobile, and David surveyed the back lot with caution before entering the decrepit shack. The room had been ravaged. Its once-full tables were now empty and turned over, and its floor littered with numerous beer and whiskey bottles and piles of cigarette butts. The clocks were gone, except for the ones that underwent repair—set in various stages of permanent dissection. Sophia quietly examined the humble room, and David wondered if it was a similar experience to the one he underwent at his mother's tenement.

"Someone has ransacked the place," David said. "They have stolen his things."

"Did they take my box?"

David knelt at the side of the cot and reached beneath it. The humble wooden munitions box, undetected by the home's intruders, was still there. He lifted it out and placed it on the cot. The box was held shut by a rusted padlock. David looked under the bed for a key, then, not finding one, forced his pocket knife's squat blade beneath the lock's casing and the aged wood it was mounted to and pried it free. He presented the box to Sophia, and she opened its lid, then lifted out an envelope.

For Sophia. 1893

"I was thirteen years old . . ." She put a hand over her mouth, then reached back into the box and pulled out an aged photograph—an image of an infant dressed in a long, embroidered silk gown.

"Oh, my." She turned it towards David. "This is my christening picture."

She set the photograph down and anxiously tore open the envelope. A smaller sheet was folded in half, then wrapped around the letter. She removed its accompanying typewritten note, and read it aloud.

✦

To whom it may concern.
For the price of ten cents I have transcribed this letter for a mister Lawrence (his family name has been withheld from me), a Negro, previously unknown to me, serving with the U.S. cavalry. The diction is my own. Mr. Lawrence requested that I include this memorandum as well as endeavor to make Mr. Lawrence's diction a trifle clearer for ease of reading. I accept no responsibility for any scurrilous message, mistruths, or fraud this letter may purport. I have merely acted as scribe in Mr. Lawrence's behalf.

—MR. CHARLES H. JENNINGS, ESQ.,
ALAMOGORDO, NEW MEXICO, 1877.

✦

Sophia set the note aside and opened the letter. It too was typewritten, and she commenced to read it out loud as well, but stopped after the first sentence. Tears fell down her cheeks. She handed the letter to David, then sat back in her chair, wiping back the still falling tears. David read the letter out loud.

✦

My dearest Sophia,
I do not hope that you will ever read this letter.
For if you do, your mama and papa have failed
in our duty to protect you from my identity. But
as you have learned of me, there are things you
must now know. You should know how much I
love you. A child should know their father's
love. You may ask why I was not in your life—
why it was so important to us to hide myself
from you. It is because we loved you that I gave
you up—that people would not hurt you. You
know, by now, that your papa is a Negro. Your
mama and I didn't want you to know that you
had mixed blood. We wanted you to have a life
my skin color could not offer. The world has
taken you away from me, but they cannot take
you from my heart. I did see you once. I came
and stood alongside the road where you walked
from school. Even though I had come across
half the country, when I saw you near I felt
afraid of how you might treat a strange Negro
and I wanted to turn back. You stopped and

asked me kindly if I was a stranger in town and needed some help to find my way. Do you recall? I thanked you and said I knew just where I needed to go. Back home. My heart was so proud I thought it would burst.

I never got the chance to say it to your face, but I love you my darling.

YOUR PAPA

✦

Sophia was unable to speak. David handed her back the letter, then glanced down at his watch.

"You have a train to catch," he said gently. "I guess you got your answer."

✦

Together they waited on the platform for the train's arrival. When Sophia had completed the formalities of her boarding, David handed her a leather satchel.

"What is this?"

"Some of your father's things from his cavalry days."

She peeled back the bag's flap. Inside was a cavalry belt rolled up to a brass rectangular buckle that read "US"; an ammunition pouch; a currycomb; Lawrence's troop manual; and his unit insignia—a blue and gold ensign with the words SEMPER PARATUS inscribed across a banner.

Sophia closed the bag and put it under her arm. "They sacrificed their love for me."

"Your father was a noble man."

Sophia looked at David thoughtfully. "There are people with fair complexions and beautiful faces with spirits as twisted and gnarled as a burr oak. My parents were the comely ones. The ones with the beautiful souls."

She leaned forward and kissed David on the cheek. "I will never be able to repay you for all that you have done for me and my father."

"It is I who am in debt."

As she boarded the train, she stopped and turned back and said, "Good luck with MaryAnne. I have faith that everything will work out. You've too good a heart for it not to."

⁺

At David's return to the house, he was awakened to a great sadness as he encountered MaryAnne's trunks stacked on the front porch. She had packed two additional cases of things that she was previously unable to escape with without divulging her flight. Upon entering the home, David went directly to his den and, sequestering himself inside, turned on his radio, seeking refuge in its broadcast. The Boston Symphony played Tchaikovsky's *"Pathétique,"* and, alone with his pain, David hung on each murmuring refrain, and each cry of the violin was his own. Not thirty minutes later, Mary-

Anne gently knocked on the door of his den, then entered. David turned off the set.

"I see you have packed your things."

She nodded humbly.

"What time is your train?"

She walked over to the world globe and ran her fingers across its surface, her back turned towards David.

"Not until morning. I thought I would spend tonight at the Hotel Utah."

David did not ask her why, and an uncomfortable silence filled the room.

"I wanted to say good-bye this time."

David dropped his head into his hand and sighed. It was more than a minute before he spoke. "You know, this is right where I was when I found your letter—found out that you were leaving. What a night that was—first time Catherine ever saw me drunk." He laughed cynically. "I don't know. Maybe it's good to get the wind knocked out of you from time to time."

MaryAnne's eyes moistened.

"Much has transpired since that night. Catherine gave me the letter you found at Andrea's grave. It got me to thinking that I needed to figure some things out. So I went to Chicago to find my mother. It turns out that my mother committed suicide twenty-two years ago."

"Catherine told me," MaryAnne replied softly. "I am so sorry, David."

"I have no idea who wrote the letter . . . but it's

not important. I learned what I needed to learn—
that it doesn't really matter what happened back
then. There is nothing anyone can do with the past,
except let it fade." He swallowed. "As I stood looking out over the bridge my mother jumped from, I
had this remarkable moment of clarity. Do you
know what I realized?"

MaryAnne began to tremble and did not turn, for
she did not want David to see her tears.

"I realized how much I missed you. And that all
that really matters in my life is earning your trust
and getting you back. And then I thought, I will
never get that chance, because you will never return. I understood the hopelessness my mother felt.
Because when you lose something that precious,
you have really lost. And I, too, wanted to jump."

MaryAnne began to sob quietly.

"And then I had the strangest thought. What if I
jumped? And then in some other realm I encountered Andrea and she asked me what I had done
with my life since she left. And I had to tell her that
I had thrown away everything that I loved. That
was my great epiphany, when I realized that what I
had been doing was really no different than what
my mother had done. That I had also abandoned
myself and those that depended on me. I didn't get
on a train to do it, but it was just as real." David
cleared his throat. "I haven't been the same since. I
don't know how to tell you this, because it just
sounds like I am trying to get you to stay." His
voice cracked. "And more than anything I want you

to stay . . ." He dropped his head. "No, that's wrong. More than anything I want you to want to stay."

MaryAnne suddenly turned to him, no longer able to suppress her feelings. "David, I thought you wanted me to leave. I came to see if you would take me back. I don't want to live without you." She walked to his chair and knelt down at its side. "I am sorry I broke the promise of my wedding vow—my promise to you. I was just so alone."

David put his hand under her chin and tilted it up until her eyes looked into his, and a smile grew across his face, and then hers. David embraced her, and the two fell to the floor in each other's arms. It was at this moment that Catherine walked in to inform MaryAnne that her taxi had arrived. Instead, she quietly closed the door, paid the taxi his pickup fee, and then tipped the man to carry Mary-Anne's trunks back inside the house. Her face shone with such joy that the cab driver almost felt guilty begrudging his lost fare.

CHAPTER 26

The Reunion

"There is no confection so sweet as joyful reunion."

DAVID PARKIN'S DIARY.
FEBRUARY 2, 1934

When morning came, David stirred and MaryAnne nestled tightly into his chest. "Oh, don't go, darling."

David strained to see the clock, then pulled her closer and kissed her forehead. "I told Gibbs I would meet him downtown for breakfast."

"Why?"

"He says that he has important news that he must share with me in person."

MaryAnne sighed sleepily and laced her fingers behind David's head. "What do you think it is?"

"Well, either he's quitting or he's getting married."

"He's certainly not quitting."

"Gibbs has such fear of matrimony. Could Elaine have finally persuaded him?"

"We women have our ways."

"I won't argue that." He kissed her again, then climbed out of bed. As he left the room, MaryAnne abandoned her own pillow and embraced his tightly.

✦

As the sleepy city awaited its usual wakening of street vendors and storefronts, David found Gibbs seated at a small oak table near the back of the

Temple Square coffee shop, reading the *Salt Lake Tribune*. A doughnut, a thick strip of grilled bacon, and a cup of coffee sat before him. When he saw David, he set the paper aside.

"Have you followed this trial in Detroit—those two men who murdered their landlord because he was about to evict their families?"

"I have heard talk about it."

"The jury acquitted them. They ruled it was self-defense."

"I'm not surprised. Survival is always the first law of the land."

A grey-haired waitress emerged from the kitchen, wiping her hands on her apron. She came to the table.

"What can I get for you?"

"Oatmeal and coffee." He looked at Gibbs's meal. "And a sinker."

She returned to the kitchen.

"So what is the big news?"

Gibbs paused for emphasis. "Elaine and I are getting married."

"Congratulations."

"I admit I am a little surprised at how happy I am about all this."

"Why is that? You're crazy about Elaine."

"It is just the commitment. It unnerves me."

"Then why are you taking the plunge?"

"I don't know. I guess it's about time."

"You mean she gave you an ultimatum."

"In so many words. We were outside the ZCMI

department store when she said, 'You can only window-shop for so long before someone else comes along and buys the display.'"

David laughed. "Subtle."

"She's a clever gal," Gibbs said. "I'll have my hands full." A wry smile stretched across his face. "Not a bad thought, really."

"You are smitten. Didn't you once warn me that love is the worm that conceals the hook?"

"I guess if the bait is sweet enough, you don't worry about the barb."

"I always thought it was inevitable. Have you set a date?"

"Soon. Early April. Elaine wants to hasten it."

"The weather would be better in May."

"She's claiming grounds of superstition—'marry in May, rue the day.' I think the truth is she's afraid that I might change my mind."

"Have you planned where you will hold the ceremony?"

"Not yet."

"Why not have it at the house?"

"We'd hate to be such an imposition—especially with MaryAnne just back."

"We'll be offended if you don't. Besides, Catherine loves these things. She turns into a little tyrant, bossing around the florists and caterers. She'll be thrilled."

"I'll talk to Elaine about it this evening." He glanced at his wristwatch. "It's almost nine. I best unlock the company doors." He laid down a dollar bill and stood. "I almost forgot the most important thing. I would like for you to be my best man."

"I would be honored."

Gibbs smiled. "Swell. I'll see you at work." He saluted David and walked out of the cafe.

On the dawn of Gibbs and Elaine's nuptial day, David fled the flurry of the mansion's final preparations and picked Gibbs up for breakfast, taking him to the nearby Alta Club, where the two men laughed and spoke of everything except the day, and Gibbs puffed cigars with the anxiousness befitting a bridegroom. They returned to the house twenty minutes before the scheduled event.

Spring, in Utah, more times than not, arrives in winter dress, and the wedding day was not excepted. The morning was clear and chill, and in preparation of the reception, the home's fires were all stoked and small heaps of firewood were raised near each hearth.

The house had been consigned as Catherine's canvas, and she spared no stroke in bringing forth her masterpiece. Every pillar on the main floor was wrapped in long foliage garnishes and vines, and the chandeliers were so adorned with flowers that they looked more bouquet than fixture.

The bride herself was not outdone by the surroundings, and it was remarked, in compliment, that Elaine resembled a Gibson girl. She wore an ivory satin and lace bridal gown of her mother's, with a high-necked bodice, full puff sleeves, and a long flared skirt with a tightly fitted waistline. As natural as the apparel took to Elaine, or she to it, Gibbs was conversely out of his element; his black cotton pants hung long, and his jacket was wrinkled from repeated fidgeting and removal.

The ceremony was held in the drawing room, and the double doors were opened to the vestibule for additional guests. The justice of the peace began the service at the strike of noon, and it proceeded quickly and unspectacularly, which suited everyone, and before the hour waned the couple was joined in matrimony. When the two were declared as one, MaryAnne dabbed her eyes with a lace handkerchief, and David squeezed her hand.

"I have never understood why it is that women cry at weddings."

"I have seen men cry, too."

"Yes. But only the grooms."

MaryAnne laughed. It had been a long time since David had teased her about anything. "You're terrible," she said happily.

At the conclusion of the service, the party moved into the foyer and downstairs parlor while tables were brought in and lunch was served.

When lunch was eaten and all had paid their respects to the newlyweds, the couple drove off beneath a hail of rice, and Catherine returned to her relentless tyranny of the caterers. The food was boxed and stored in the pantry, while several boxes of cake, sliced meats, and breadstuffs were sent to the breadlines for the homeless.

When the last of the guests had departed, David and MaryAnne walked up the stairs hand in hand.

"Honestly, are you surprised to see them married?" MaryAnne asked.

"No. In fact I wonder that it didn't happen sooner." David kissed her. "It brings back fond memories, doesn't it?"

"This day has been healing. I feel as if I had been reliving our own wedding day."

Suddenly, MaryAnne paused. She stood outside the parlor and looked at the door. David watched her. Hoping. Wondering if she would enter to see the clock he had given her on their wedding day.

"What is it, Mary?"

She turned away. "Nothing."

At the entrance of their bedroom, David stopped her.

"Wait here. I want to show you something."

He entered the darkened room, then returned with a small, wrapped package and handed it to her.

"What is this?"

"I never gave you a Christmas present."

MaryAnne smiled. "But it's April, David." She curiously weighed the box in her hands, as it felt empty. As she tore back the paper, David switched on the room's lights. To the side of the turned-down bed were two trunks. She glanced at them, then back into David's face.

"Why are the trunks out?"

"Finish opening your present and you'll know."

She opened the package to reveal two card tickets. David slipped his arms around her waist. "It has been too long since we have been away together. I thought a holiday to San Francisco was in order."

"David." She pressed against him.

"Catherine has packed for you. I have reserved seats on an airplane flight for tomorrow morning."

"An airplane flight? How exciting."

"I thought we'd stay at the Palace Hotel and spend a few days on the Barbary Coast. Perhaps sail to Tiburon for lunch at Sam's."

"Oh, David. It will be wonderful. We could see Grass Valley again."

David's demeanor fell at the suggestion. He looked at her gravely. "No, MaryAnne. There is nothing left for me there."

Still encircled in his arms, she leaned back to look into his face.

"Nothing?"

"I have wasted too much time in Grass Valley."

"But you haven't been there in twenty-five years."

"A part of me had never left it. It's time to move on."

She lay her head against his chest. "You really are back, my love."

"With all of my vulnerable heart. Do with it as you will."

She held him tighter and knew that she would never let him go.

"I will hold it tightly next to mine."

✦

David sat alone at a table on the wood-planked pier, drinking orange juice and reading from the *San Francisco Examiner.* A glass bowl of fruit— oranges and pomegranates—stood centerpiece on the white wrought-iron table next to a book and a folded cardigan. The wharf stretched out beneath the dawn California sun over the kelp-strewn beach of Sausalito Bay. The barking of sea lions re- sounded from a distant rock, above the seagulls' desperate screech—the ocean's cacophony carried on the breeze that swept in from the bay and ruffled MaryAnne's wraparound skirt as she walked from their room towards David.

David tilted the paper to watch his beautiful wife approach. MaryAnne looked younger than she had in years—the weight of his remorse lifted. She smiled demurely at his glance as she pulled back the strands of hair that the wind blew in her face.

"Good morning, my dear," David said.

"This is glorious, David." She sat down next to him. "I just love the smell of the ocean."

He leaned over and kissed her. "What can I order you for breakfast?"

"I'll just have fruit." She took an orange from the bowl. "This is just like our honeymoon."

"With much in common. It is a whole new life we have ahead of us." He set aside the paper and looked at MaryAnne with peculiar gravity. "Maybe we should start our new life here in California."

She laid a piece of rind on the table. "What are you saying, David?"

"I have been thinking. There is really no reason to go back to Salt Lake. Lawrence is gone. Gibbs is starting his family. He can certainly run the business without me."

"You are serious?"

"Why not? The snow seems a little higher and colder each year. Maybe it's time to retire to some-place more temperate."

"But our home . . . and Catherine."

"Catherine could come with us."

"We couldn't ask her to come."

"Of course we could. And she would. We're as much family to her as she is to us."

"But our home . . ."

"Mary." David smiled as he looked into her eyes. "Wherever you are is home."

MaryAnne was suddenly quiet. A line of pelicans flew by, and MaryAnne's eyes followed their roller-coaster flight.

"Are you worried about leaving Andrea?" David asked.

"No. Not anymore. It doesn't matter where we go. I carry her with me always."

"If you don't like the idea . . ."

"The idea of change is always hard. But I have always wanted to live by the coast. Perhaps a beach home in Monterey." She suddenly smiled with new excitement. "I think we should, David. Maybe this summer."

"I wonder what Gibbs will say?"

"He'll be heartbroken. The two of you are like brothers."

"Closer than brothers. He's the only one who has seen me through it all." David suddenly smiled. "Of course it's Victoria I really worry about."

MaryAnne laughed heartily, and David reflected on how sweet that laughter sounded and could not imagine that he had lived without it for so long.

"Oh, David. What will the woman do without you?"

CHAPTER 27

The Sexton's Call

"The noble causes of life have always seemed foolish to the uninspired. But this is of small concern. I worry less about the crucified than those who pounded the nails."

DAVID PARKIN'S DIARY.
MARCH 4, 1934

MaryAnne felt David's forehead for the fifth time. "It's the change in climate, David. Last week you were swimming in the ocean and today you are out shoveling snow." She sighed. "I had better stay," she decided.

David caught her hand. "I'll be fine. This is the troupe's last performance. I want you to go with Gibbs and Elaine."

Catherine entered the room. "Gibbs just arrived. Shall I tell him to go on without you?"

"No," David said adamantly, "Mary is going."

MaryAnne looked vexed. "I did want to see this opera."

"There is no sense in you missing it because I have a cold."

The sound of a brass knocker reverberated through the house, followed by that of the opening door.

David coughed. "Now go on. You know how impatient Gibbs gets."

MaryAnne kissed David's forehead. "You stay in bed. Catherine, we will be at the Capitol Theater. We should be back no later than midnight."

"Enjoy yourself," Catherine said. "Everything will be fine."

Gibbs stalked into the room, and his eyes fell on David. "What are you doing in bed?"

"David is ill," Catherine said. "Now go, Mary. You're making everyone late."

"Thank you, Catherine." She kissed David. "Good night, darling."

Gibbs slapped David's knee. "I tried to get out of it myself."

David smiled. "I am sure you will tell me all about it."

When they had left the room, Catherine smiled at David. "May I get you anything?"

"Hot tea would be nice."

"I found some Jeelung at the store." She descended to the kitchen, returning a quarter hour later with the tea service. She set it at the side of the bed.

"Is it true that oranges and avocados grow alongside the roads in California?"

David smiled at Catherine's childlike wonderment. "It is. Though most of them have high fences around them. Haven't you ever been to California?"

"I have never been outside of Utah."

"We are so happy that you are going with us. In truth, we would not have gone without you."

Catherine smiled. "Nor would I have let you."

"The three of us should go look for a home later this month."

Catherine's face showed her excitement. "I have always wanted to see San Francisco."

She sighed happily as she stood. "I told MaryAnne that you would rest. Would you like the light off?"

"No. I'll read."

Catherine went back downstairs to the laundry. Two hours later the telephone rang. Catherine answered, then, a few moments later, peered in to see if David was awake.

"David, it is for you. It is the sexton of the city cemetery."

David lifted the receiver. "Hello."

The man's excited voice resonated from the earpiece, and David's countenance turned grave. Catherine tried to ascertain the crisis from David's contribution to the conversation.

"How did they know of it? . . . And the police?"

There was a long pause, and the concern on David's face was more manifest. "I will be right there."

David moved the phone from his ear, and Catherine took the handset from him to hang it up.

"You will be right where?"

"A group of men have gathered at the cemetery to dig up Lawrence's grave."

"Good Lord."

David swung his legs over the side of the bed. "I need to get up there."

Catherine lifted the handset. "I'll call the police."

"No," David said. He suddenly doubled over in a fit of coughing. Then, straightening up, he walked to the wardrobe and pulled on a pair of trousers, tucking his nightshirt into the waist. "The grave is illegal. The police won't stop the men."

"Illegal?"

"It's against the law to bury a Negro in the cemetery. I knew it when I purchased the plot."

David continued to dress.

"Please do not go."

"I can't let them do this."

Catherine wrung her hands. "Are you going to take your gun?"

"That would be foolishness."

"Then please wait for Gibbs to return."

"It will be over by the time he returns." He finished lacing his boots. "I am just going to see if I can talk them out of it." He took a wad of bills from the nightstand drawer and stashed it in a trouser pocket. "And, if that doesn't work, bribe them out of it. It will be all right."

He walked out of the room and descended the stairway with Catherine at his heels. "You shouldn't be out in this cold. Your cough . . ."

"I will only be a few minutes."

She brought out his long coat from the hall closet. "Take your good coat."

He slipped on the coat and buttoned it down, then opened the front door, ushering in a rush of freezing air. Catherine shuddered.

"What will I tell MaryAnne?"

"MaryAnne needn't know. I'll be back long before she is."

"David, I am afraid. What if something goes wrong?" Their eyes met. "Aren't you afraid?"

He thought momentarily, then said, "I am afraid of many things."

✦

David climbed the snow-capped western hill of the cemetery, creeping unseen through the shadows cast by the great canopies of oak. From a distance he could hear the excited sounds of the men, occasional laughter, and the rhythmic hit of shovels. He increased his gait. When he arrived, above the knoll, the grave had already been dug down three feet past ground level. There were no more than a dozen men gathered on the trampled snow, and the knoll was lit by two kerosene lanterns resting on the base of Andrea's grave. Two men, perspiration dripping down their faces despite the cold, flung dirt out of the cavity while the others shouted their encouragement. The shovelers' jackets were draped over the angel statue's head and outstretched arms. Despite the frigid climate, it was fast digging, for the dirt was still loose from the recent burial, and three men leaned idly against their pickaxes while the shovels did the work, heaping dirt on both sides of the grave. As the hole grew, so did their delirium, and they mocked the buried man and made plans of what they would do with his corpse once it was exhumed. The guttural talk turned David's stomach. He shouted into the commotion.

"Stop!"

The voices abated. His voice took on a calmer resonance.

"Please, stop."

A burly, barrel-chested man in a leather jacket and worker boots stepped forward. "Who are you?"

David didn't reply. Just then a small ruddy-faced man stepped from the crowd.

"It's Parkin. He's the nigger-lover who buried this here jig."

David faced his accuser, and the man cowered back into the shadows.

"Judd?"

"There are niggers takin' white men's wages, and it ain't right. Man's got a right to protect his family."

"How does a buried man threaten your families?"

The behemoth scowled. "This is what's the problem, right here. A bunch of high-hat nigger lovers giving the darkies our families' bread. Real high and mighty sermon preachin' comin' from a cake eater. I spit at you." At that the man spat in David's direction, then wiped the spittle from his mouth with his coat sleeve. "When the last time your children cried themselves asleep a hungered?"

The question evoked more feeling than the inquirer could have imagined. David held his silence.

"I say we show this high hat how we feels about darky-lovers."

David stood motionless as several of the men advanced.

"I have no quarrel with any of you. The man buried here was my friend."

"Maybe you got the wrong friends."

"Yeah," chimed another, "in low places."

The men chortled, then a cry went up. "Get him!"

David was quickly set upon by more than a half dozen of the brood. Two held his arms while another struck him across the face and then in the abdomen. When they released David from their grasp, he fell to his side on the icy ground, clutching his ribs and gasping for breath. A trickle of blood gathered at the base of his chin and dyed the snow crimson. One of the men who had held his arms spit on him.

"Hey. No use soilin' that fancy coat. Coat like that fetch a dollar or two."

Two of his assailants pulled the coat from his back, while another pushed his face in the snow with his boot.

"Look at this pantywaist, wearin' a nightgown underneath."

The man holding the coat suddenly shouted. "Hey, there's money here. Drinks tonight." In celebration, he kicked David in the side. At that moment another swaggered up to him, carrying a decapitated pick handle, which he unceremoniously swung down on David's head. Unconscious and face forward in the snow, the men were no longer entertained by his presence. They left him and returned to the grave and their original designs. David was still unconscious when the triumphant shout went up as the first shovel struck the wooden top of the casket. He never saw the imbeciles haul the coffin from the pit or load it into the wood-planked bed of a battered pickup truck and cart it away.

✦

The foyer clock had struck midnight nearly a half hour earlier when MaryAnne, Elaine, and Gibbs returned. It had been more than two hours since David had left the home. Catherine rushed out to meet them.

"David went up to the cemetery to stop some men from digging up Lawrence's grave. He left hours ago and he hasn't returned."

"Dear God," MaryAnne exclaimed.

Gibbs shoved the car back into gear while MaryAnne shouted for Catherine to call Dr. Twede and then the police. They raced up to the cemetery. The cemetery gates were still open from the men's hasty departure, and a broken chain lay coiled against the curbway. Gibbs careened between the black, narrow cemetery trails. When the angel came into view, they could see the muddy, trampled snow of the knoll and the gaping hole in the earth where Lawrence had once lain. Near the top of the knoll the car's headlights exposed a small heap. As they neared, MaryAnne gasped. "It is David."

Gibbs braked to a stop, and MaryAnne threw her door open. She ran to her husband's body.

"He is still breathing."

"Where is his coat?" Elaine screamed. Gibbs lifted David and carried him to the car, nearly dropping him into the backseat. MaryAnne covered David's frigid body with hers as they sped back to the house. MaryAnne did not stop praying the whole way.

✦

Around noon the next day, Dr. Twede stood in the doorway of the bedchamber rubbing his neck. His awkward, lanky frame seemed dwarfed in the white smock he wore, and a stethoscope fell to his buckle. MaryAnne left David's side to speak with him.

"He was beaten quite severely. He has a concussion from a blow to his head. I am surprised that I haven't found any broken bones."

"Will he be all right?"

"His wounds from the beating will be all right. The exposure is what concerns me. He is running a very high fever. He was already ill. I am afraid it has turned to pneumonia."

MaryAnne shuddered at the pronouncement. "What can we do?"

"Just what we are," he replied. "And pray."

Despite MaryAnne's prayers, David's condition continued to worsen, and though he was lucid, by nightfall his fever had risen another two degrees. Gibbs walked into David's room holding his hat to his waist.

"David, Captain Brookes himself has come. Your overcoat has been recovered. He needs your help to identify the men who beat you."

David looked up thoughtfully, then slowly nodded. His words were slurred and spoken slowly. "No, Gibbs."

"But why not, David?"

"What could come of it but to spawn more hatred?"

Gibbs was incredulous. "Justice will come of it. David, it was you that spoke of justice."

David nodded. "I have said too much on the topic." He looked at his friend seriously. "Let the anger go, Gibbs. There will be justice."

Gibbs sighed at David's obstinance.

"What became of Lawrence's grave?"

"They took the coffin to a field and set it afire." Gibbs had shared only half of what he knew. He could no longer restrain himself. "Why did you put yourself in such danger for the Negroes?"

David took a deep, troubled breath. "I didn't do it for the Negroes. What happened that night is imperceptible on the pile of injustices heaped upon the Negroes. I do it for my own race, not theirs."

"For what purpose? You couldn't have stopped them."

"Perhaps not. But to not try would make me seem absurd in my own eyes."

The conversation collapsed into silence. After a minute David spoke again. "The papers were signed long ago for you to take over the business. We haven't always seen eye to eye, Gibbs. But you have always been a loyal friend." He was interrupted by a fit of coughing. He took a breath, then a drink from a tumbler from the nearby nightstand. "I have deeded half the business to you, the other half to MaryAnne. Promise me that you will always take care of Mary."

Gibbs looked frantic. "What are you insinuating?"

"Just promise me, Gibbs."

Gibbs's chin began to quiver. "I give you my word."

"Then I will worry no more of the matter."

The two men embraced, and as Gibbs walked to the doorway, David stopped him. "Gibbs."

"Yes, David."

"You are my brother."

Gibbs lowered his head and walked out of the room.

＊

By nightfall of the second day, a fatigued and greatly distressed doctor spoke with MaryAnne and Catherine in the hallway outside David's room.

"His lips have started to turn blue. He is not getting the oxygen he needs. The severity of his chest pain has increased as well. We can try chlorine gas, but, in honesty, I have not seen any evidence of it helping."

"Are you saying that my husband is dying?"

The doctor frowned. "I am not certain of that. I just want you to be prepared. If there is anything you need to say, it might be a good time."

MaryAnne suddenly began to hyperventilate. Catherine quickly led her to a chair. The doctor waited for her to gain her composure. "I am sorry, MaryAnne. I will be back in the morning." The doctor stopped once more in the room. He laid his hand on David's forehead. His own forehead creased, and he said under his breath, "Good-bye, old sport."

When she had regained her composure, Mary-Anne returned to David's bedside. The bedchamber's fire crackled and hissed, lighting the room with its dancing radiance. David's lips were covered with fever blisters, and to MaryAnne's dismay grew more discolored by the hour. His skin grew wan and transparent. At a half hour past two o'clock in the morning, Catherine entered the room. She spoke in hushed tones.

"MaryAnne, you must get some rest. I will come for you if he wakes. Even for a moment."

MaryAnne glanced up wearily, too tired to resist, and Catherine helped her up and out to another room, then took her place in the oak chair beside the bed. She thumbed through the pages of a book, turning pages without garnishing a thought. David's voice startled her.

"Catherine." The voice was slurred and gurgled.

"Yes?"

"Where's Mary?"

"I sent her to rest. I will wake her."

"No . . ." He succumbed to a tortured coughing fit, and Catherine grimaced with each fierce bark. ". . . I want to talk to you first."

She leaned close, her torso overhanging the bed.

"I want to say good-bye."

Catherine recoiled at his words. "No. It is not come to that."

"Catherine."

She began to shake and cupped her face in her hands.

"Catherine . . . ," he said still harder, the outburst causing him to again erupt in a fit of coughing. She looked back up at him.

". . . it has come to that."

Catherine could say nothing as tears began to fall.

"I want to thank you for the years of love and service."

"I should never have let you go out," she cried.

"Don't you blame yourself." Again he coughed, this time for nearly a full minute. When he could talk again, he spoke meekly. "You couldn't have stopped me."

She bowed her head again.

"You once spoke of angels guiding us. I believe that you have been my guardian angel."

Her whimpering grew into uncontrollable sobs. "What will I do without you, David?"

He motioned for her to draw near, and he leaned forward and kissed her forehead. The motion caused his head to spin, and he fell back into his pillow.

"Wake Mary."

Catherine nodded, stood, wiping back her tears with her sleeve. She paused at the doorway. "David . . ."

"Good-bye."

She tried to return his farewell, but the attempt was abandoned by her faltering voice. She dropped her head and walked from the room. A moment later MaryAnne entered, dressed in the cotton gown she had worn the day before, though it was crinkled as she had lain in it, and she pushed it down to lessen its severity. She clutched a crumpled handkerchief in her hand. Her skin was wan, a pallid white accented by her red-rimmed nostrils and eyes—further darkened by her drought of sleep. She walked to the side of his bed and sat down wearily beside him. He forced a smile when he saw her. For reasons she could not explain, she turned away from his gaze. Still looking down she asked, "How do you feel, love?"

He coughed again, and purposely did not answer.

"Shall I stoke the fire?"

He modestly shook his head. "No."

"Ethan has wired. He is coming from London. He is bringing Charlotta . . ."

David just continued to gaze on her, catching the rise and fall of each word and tasting her voice. MaryAnne shuddered, then fell to her knees and cried, "Why, when I would pour out my whole heart, am I babbling of such trivial matters?"

David's voice was full of consolation. "The moment speaks for itself."

MaryAnne braved to look into his eyes. Then, suddenly, the moment flooded into her like a torrential current filling her entire soul to the extent of her heart's capacity.

"You cannot leave me, David. You cannot. I just got you back." She broke down in desperate sobs. "Please don't leave me."

David put his hand around the back of her head and pulled it into his waist, and he, too, cried.

"Not just yet."

He began choking, and MaryAnne looked up helplessly, squeezing his hand. He suddenly breathed in again, and his body relaxed. MaryAnne's heart pounded.

"David. Take me with you."

"It's not your time, Mary. Andrea and I will await you. I am convinced of that."

"And what if not? What if there is nothing after?"

He gazed silently into MaryAnne's pained eyes, then answered, "With you, I would do it again."

"Oh, David," she sobbed. Clinging desperately to

the man she loved, she buried her head into his body and wept until the bed's wooden frame rocked with her convulsions. David held her hand. His grip gradually relaxed as the relentless pull of fatigue seduced him. MaryAnne's weeping also began to still, her murmuring softened until the only motion of her body was the gentle rise and fall of her breathing. He coughed hard, and her head rose.

"I am sorry, David. I am so tired."

He touched her hair and wanted nothing more than to spare her the pain of his leaving. "Rest, Mary. It is late."

"What if . . ." The words froze in her throat.

"I will be here in the dawn." He closed his eyes, and MaryAnne laid her head on his body and also closed hers.

The home was dark and quiet. The room's hearth grew dimmer, and the chamber's only steady light was a single, small bulb from the nightstand's lamp. Nearly an hour later, David was again woken by coughing, but this time something was different, and he knew that his body had entered a final phase of digression. He looked on MaryAnne. Her head now rested against his waist, only partially concealing the graceful curves of the face that had first drawn his eye and then his heart. He realized that he had seen that face only a few times in his life, for he had replaced it with an image of something far deeper than physical attraction. He stretched forth his hand to her head and took the tousled, umber strands between his fingers. He spoke to her in whispers as she slept.

"Could we not have spent just a few more minutes?"

Tears began to fall down his cheeks as he struggled to breathe. But they were not tears of pain, but separation. His chest seemed to be constricting more tightly now, and each breath had to be bargained for. A spasm caught him, and he clenched with its pain, his breath turning to pants. When it had passed, he looked back longingly at the woman at his side. It was time.

"I love you, MaryAnne Parkin. I have always loved you."

His chest constricted again, and he grimaced with its contraction.

"Must I go alone?" He struggled to catch another breath, then, unable once more to cough up the fluids that filled his lungs, surrendered his last word. "Mary . . ."

At eleven minutes past four, David Parkin died. There was no one awake to note the hour of David's passing. When dawn came, awakening the city in its golden radiance, a wail echoed through the corridors of the great Parkin house, and Catherine, running to the aid of her mistress, entered the room, where she found MaryAnne on her knees, clutching her husband's waist and sobbing.

Carousels

"From our first babblings to our last word, we make but one statement, and that is our life."

DAVID PARKIN'S DIARY.
OCTOBER 11, 1933

Another cavity was opened on the cemetery's knoll, and the stone angel's shadow trespassed the simple granite marker that denoted the resting place of David Parkin. By one o'clock, a crowd of considerable body had gathered for the eulogy. Every living worker at the Parkin Machinery Company, current and retired, attended with spouse and family—a tribute to David's great heart.

At the side of the casket, Catherine and MaryAnne, in ebony attire, held each other in disbelief, as if it all were some ghastly drama.

Inconspicuously, to one side of the gathering, stood a quorum of Negroes who had braved stigma to pay homage to a white man they considered a friend. Gibbs stood to Catherine's side, with Elaine by his. An Episcopalian minister, young and flaxen-haired, newly ordained to the diocese, stood at the head of the casket, reading his eulogy from a worn prayer book that was not his own.

"O God, whose mercies cannot be numbered, accept our prayers on behalf of thy servant David and grant him entrance into the land of light and joy, in the fellowship of thy saints; through Jesus Christ thy Son our Lord, who liveth and reigneth with thee and the Holy Spirit, one God, now and forever. Amen."

MaryAnne stepped forward and placed a flower and a gold pocket watch on the casket's hood before it was lowered into the earth.

Gibbs put his arm around MaryAnne's waist. "I promised David that I would take care of you. I am always here for you, Mary."

She embraced him. "Thank you, Gibbs. He loved you."

At this, Gibbs swallowed and his eyes further moistened. Elaine buried her face into his shoulder.

As the mourners congregated to pay their respects to MaryAnne, a young woman, dressed in an elegant black silk gown, stepped forward to the new widow. A veil fell from the woman's bowler hat, partially concealing a beautiful and youthful countenance, now florid with grief.

"Mrs. Parkin, I wanted to share my condolences."

"Thank you, dear," MaryAnne replied. She looked closely into the stranger's face. "Forgive me, I do not remember you."

"We have never met. My name is Dierdre Williams. I was an acquaintance of David's."

"Thank you for coming."

Dierdre started to turn away, then suddenly paused. She looked back into the widow's face. "You are fortunate to have been loved such."

MaryAnne's sad stare flashed with bewilderment as the young woman turned and walked away to join up with her aunt.

As the last of the crowd dispersed, Catherine took MaryAnne's arm. "Let's go home, Mary."

MaryAnne just stared at the marker for a moment, then bowed her head. "I would like to be alone for a while."

Catherine took her hand. "I shall come back for you."

"I will walk home."

Gibbs embraced MaryAnne once more, then took Elaine's hand and departed the knoll, followed closely by Catherine.

It was only a few moments after the crowd's silent departure when an elderly woman, hunched with age, advanced slowly from behind the trees. MaryAnne recalled having seen the feeble woman standing afar from the crowd and had dismissed her as a visitor to another grave. The woman looked at her as if she would speak, then turned to the marker, knelt down, and placed a small wooden object next to a single red rose. She remained on her knees. She was heavyset and disheveled, her tattered clothes, like their wearer, a remnant of a bygone era. Her silver hair was tousled, pulled back in a careless bun.

MaryAnne felt herself drawn to the woman who knelt at her husband's grave. The woman, aware of MaryAnne's gaze, looked up. Her face was ancient and creased in wrinkles. Yet there was something familiar in her face—something MaryAnne had seen before. And then, in the woman's deep-set eyes, she saw David.

"Rose . . . ?"

The woman gazed at her, her silence neither confirming nor denying.

"You are David's mother."

The woman remained silent. MaryAnne could not help but feel apprehension in the woman's presence.

"Are you . . . real?"

She struggled to her feet, then replied in a solemn, coarse voice. "You are David's wife?"

"Yes."

"What is your name?"

"MaryAnne."

"MaryAnne," she repeated, nodding slowly. "My David married beautiful." She looked down, and the wind caught the hair at the nape of her neck.

"He went back to Chicago to find you."

A strange, sad smile lit her lips. "They think I'm a ghost, in Chicago. I have read that I haunt a theater there." She spoke the words with peculiar indifference. "Tell me about my son."

"He was loving and strong and loyal."

"Everything I am not."

MaryAnne just stared at the wretched woman. "How long have you been here? In the valley?"

"Months," she answered tersely.

"Why didn't you come to see David?"

The woman didn't answer, but suddenly glanced from side to side as if someone had joined them. "You pity me, perhaps. Or maybe hate me."

"Yes, I pity you. For what you traded away. For

what you might have known. But I do not hate you."

"You wondered that I was a ghost?"

"I was told you had died," MaryAnne said.

"I am dead to all I have known. To everyone I have known. I roam this world in regret of all that might have been. Dead or not, I am a ghost. I never jumped from that bridge. Looking out over that black water . . ." She paused as if the very memory held terror still. "It should be of no surprise to anyone. My whole life I never fulfilled any promise. Even my dying. It is my curse, to live to lose my son twice." She suddenly stirred from her own mumbling. "I did not come to mourn my son. I lost him a lifetime ago. I came to mourn my choices. And meet one promise." Rose looked down at the offering she had left on his marker—a wooden toy carousel.

MaryAnne sniffed and brushed at her cheek, and the woman abruptly said, "You haven't the right to sorrow. You have had so much."

The words enraged MaryAnne. "So much to have lost. Everything I held dear is now only a memory."

"Memories are what we trade our mortality for. What I would do for just memories."

"Even when they bring such pain?"

Fresh tears fell down MaryAnne's cheek, but the woman only glared at her. Her hard countenance revealed no sympathy. "There are worse things than pain."

To her own surprise, MaryAnne's heart welled,

no longer for herself, but for the austere soul of this woman. Unexpectedly, a single tear fell down the hard woman's cheek, and it rolled slowly like a drop of rain on cracked, baked desert clay. "Everyone dies. You have lived. You shan't ask for more."

A gust of wind swept through the grounds in a sudden breath, and the evergreens quivered while the smaller ones bowed in condescension. MaryAnne pulled the scarf up around her chin. "Will you come back with me? To our home?"

There was a sudden change to the woman's demeanor, and her reply came as if she spoke only to herself—answering voices only she heard.

"I do not belong here."

"Where will you go?"

"Away!" And at the word, she looked off in the distance as if her soul had already fled, followed longingly by her gaze. "Away from this miserable cold. To California. It is warm in California . . ."

She began to nod as if she had arrived at consensus with the spirits that shared her soul. She spoke with a voice inadequate to express the lesson her words conveyed. ". . . we were always warm in California."

At this, the old woman turned abruptly and shuffled off without farewell—having forgotten that she had shared in conversation with someone now left behind. MaryAnne's gaze followed her until the hunched form fell from view below the stone fence that divided the cemetery. MaryAnne stepped to the grave, then stooped and lifted the toy

carousel with both hands. It was a simple wooden
toy, crudely carved and painted, yet capable of pro-
ducing such wonder in a child as to define an age.
Despite the simple workmanship, it was not unlike
the toy carousel David had brought back for Andrea more than two decades earlier when she was
still an infant. She wondered if David had consciously remembered the toy when he had purchased it for his child and if seeing it had brought
him the joy of remembrance or the pain of loss. Or,
instead, if something deep inside, forgotten to the
waken mind but etched on the tablets of his heart,
had drawn him to the carousel, to give his child a
symbol of his commitment to her—that he, like the
toy, would never leave.

MaryAnne stowed the carousel under her cloak
and carried it back to the home. She climbed the
stairway to the second floor of the mansion. In her
hand she held a skeleton key she thought she would
never use again. In the other hand was the wooden
toy.

She unlocked the door, then, taking a deep
breath, pushed the parlor door open. Like David
had been, she, too, was lost in the sudden outflow
of memories the sight evoked. She had forgotten
how beautiful the room had once been and, though
cloaked in a shroud of dust, still was. Her eyes
were immediately drawn to the bed and then to the
grandfather's clock, remembering the day of its
birth as well as its death.

On the fireplace mantel across the room, she

found what she had come for—the delicate porcelain carousel David had given to Andrea. She gently brushed the dust from the piece, revealing its intricate pastel and gilt markings. She released the toy's catch and the porcelain carousel turned, its horses rose and fell to the sweet, gentle melody of its music box, then abruptly stopped, its spring unwound. The wooden carousel did not match the beauty of Andrea's exquisite toy, yet the connection was undeniable.

MaryAnne sat down on the parlor's dusty carpet, gazing at the two small toys she cradled in her lap. She wound the smooth silver key of the music box, and the tines again filled the air of the once dead room with the carnival sounds of life. And she wept for the loss of her love.

✦ EPILOGUE ✦

ourteen years after her husband's death, MaryAnne Parkin was buried next to David and Andrea on the knoll of the angel statue. It was at her funeral that I met the remaining survivor of the era—Catherine. Catherine had married four years after David's death and, with MaryAnne's blessings and tears, moved with her new husband to the temperate climate of the small township of St. George, Utah, south of the great red rock monuments of Zion Canyon. Despite the distance, she spoke with MaryAnne each week, and, we discovered, knew much of Keri and me from MaryAnne's letters.

Catherine was petite of stature, as small as Keri, with blond hair turned grey that fell to her shoulders but no further. She had captivating hazel eyes, mimicking her hair's adopted hue, dramatic and tear-shaped like a fawn's. Noticeably, she was attentive to all about her as one who has spent her life

in service often becomes. She spoke fondly of
MaryAnne and the life they had shared, and she
questioned us considerably about our stay. I sensed
in her query a longing for the mansion and an earlier time, if but to capture again a single note of the
sweet song of a day gone by.

The marble angel statue stands to this day in the
Salt Lake City cemetery, midway through the
graveyard on Center Street, amidst the willows and
sycamores, just above the ground called Babyland,
where children are buried. Our family visits the
statue each Christmas season, and during one yule
visit, our second daughter, Allyson, pointed out a
peculiar thing. During the holiday months, the sun
at the angel's back so lights the statue that its
shadow spreads its wings over the three graves, and
the family is united again in the seraph's embrace.
If it appears to be a small thing, it is still of beauty.
And nothing of beauty is insignificant.

MaryAnne and David Parkin left us many things
of beauty, the greatest of which are their lessons of
love and life—lessons that time will never forget,
nor diminish. David's death was not in vain, for, as
he once himself wrote, "life is the greatest of all
statements," and in his great sacrifice he spoke vol-
umes, showing us that there are things not only
worth dying for, but, more importantly, worth living for. For life's greatest philosophy is not handed
down in stoic texts and dusty tomes, but lived, in
each breath and act of human compassion. For love

has always demanded sacrifice, and no greater love is there than that for which our lives are traded.

And in this great cause of spiritual evolution we are all called to be martyrs, to die each of us in the quest of a higher realm and loftier ideals, that we may know God.

And what if there is nothing else? What if all life ends in the silent void of death? Then is it all in vain? I think not. For love, for the sake of love, will always be enough. And if our lives are but a single flash in the dark hollow of eternity, then, if, but for the briefest of moments, we shine—then how brilliantly our light has burned. And as the starlight knows no boundary of space or time, so, too, our illumination will shine forth throughout all eternity, for darkness has no power to quell such light. And this is a lesson we must all learn and take to heart— that all light is eternal and all love is light. And it must forever be so.

Richard Paul Evans is the best-selling author of *The Christmas Box* and *Timepiece*. He lives in Salt Lake City, Utah, with his wife, Keri, and their three daughters, Jenna, Allyson, and Abigail. He is currently working on his next novel. Keri is currently working on their next baby.